ELEMENTALS

THE PROPHECY OF SHADOWS

michelle madow

ALSO BY MICHELLE MADOW

The Elementals Series
The Prophecy of Shadows
The Blood of the Hydra (coming April 2016)

The Transcend Time Saga
Remembrance
Vengeance
Timeless

The Secret Diamond Sisters Trilogy
The Secret Diamond Sisters
Diamonds in the Rough
Diamonds are Forever

DEDICATION

To Kaitlin, for being an amazing roomie while I wrote
the first draft of this book!

In the beginning of the new year, the Olympian Comet will cross the sky and the wall will grow thin. Five representing each part of the world will work together to restore the balance, the power of the Aether igniting them. The Journey will lead them East on the path to the Shadows, which will serve as their guide.

-Written on June 2, 1692 by Abigail Goode in Kinsley, Massachusetts.

CHAPTER ONE

The secretary fumbled through the stacks of papers on her desk, searching for my schedule. "Here it is." She pulled out a piece of paper and handed it to me. "I'm Mrs. Dopkin. Feel free to come to me if you have any questions."

"Thanks." I looked at the schedule, which had my name on the top, and listed my classes and their locations. "This can't be right." I held it closer, as if that would make it change. "It has me in all honors classes."

She frowned and clicked around her computer. "Your schedule is correct," she said. "Your homeroom teacher specifically requested that you be in the honors courses."

"But I wasn't in honors at my old school."

"It doesn't appear to be a mistake," she said. "And the late bell's about to ring, so if you need a schedule adjustment, come back at the end of the day so we can discuss it. You're in Mr. Faulkner's homeroom, in the library. Turn right out of the office and walk down the hall. You'll see the library on the right. Go inside and head all the way to the back. Your homeroom is in the only door there. Be sure to hurry—you don't want to be late."

She returned to her computer, apparently done talking to me, so I thanked her for her help and left the office.

Kinsley High felt cold compared to my school in Georgia, and not just in the literal sense. Boxy tan lockers lined every wall, and the concrete floor was a strange mix of browns that reminded me of throw-up. The worst part was that there were no windows anywhere, and therefore a serious lack of sunlight.

I preferred the warm green carpets and open halls at my old school. Actually I preferred everything about my small Georgia town, especially the sprawling house and the peach tree farm I left behind. But I tried not to complain too much to my parents.

After all, I remembered the way my dad had bounced around the living room while telling us about his promotion to anchorman on the news station. It was his dream job, and he didn't mind that the only position available was in Massachusetts. My mom had jumped on board with the plan to move, confident that her paintings would sell better in a town closer to a major city. My younger sister Becca had liked the idea of starting fresh, along with how the shopping in Boston apparently exceeded anything in our town in Georgia.

There had to be something about the move for me to like. Unfortunately, I had yet to find it.

I didn't realize I'd arrived at the library until the double doors were in front of me. At least I'd found it without getting lost.

I walked inside the library, pleased to find it was nothing like the rest of the school. The golden carpet and wooden walls were warm and welcoming, and the upstairs even had windows. I yearned to run toward the sunlight, but the late bell had already rung, so I headed to the back of the library. Hopefully being new would give me a free pass on being late.

Just as the secretary had said, there was only one door. But with it's ancient peeling wood, it looked like it led to a storage room, not a classroom. And there was no glass panel, so I couldn't peek inside. I had to assume this was it.

I wrapped my fingers around the doorknob, my hand trembling. *It's your first day*, I reminded myself. *No one's going to blame you for being late on your first day.*

I opened the door, halfway expecting it to be a closet full of old books or brooms. But it wasn't a closet.

It was a classroom.

Everyone stared at me, and I looked to the front of the room, where a tall, lanky man in a tweed suit stood next to a blackboard covered with the morning announcements. His gray hair shined under the light, and his wrinkled skin and warm smile reminded me more of a grandfather than a teacher.

He cleared his throat and rolled a piece of chalk in his palm. "You must be Nicole Cassidy," he said.

"Yeah." I nodded and looked around at the other students. There were about thirty of them, and there seemed to be an invisible line going down the middle of the room, dividing them in half. The students near the door wore jeans and sweatshirts, but the ones closer to the wall looked like they were dressed for a fashion show instead of school.

"It's nice to meet you Nicole." The teacher sounded sincere, like he was meeting a new friend instead of a student. "Welcome to our homeroom. I'm Mr. Faulkner, but please call me Darius." He turned to the chalkboard, lifted his hand, and waved it from one side to the other. "You probably weren't expecting everything to look so normal, but we have to be careful. As I'm sure you know, we can't risk letting anyone else know what goes on in here."

Then the board shimmered—like sunlight glimmering off the ocean—and the morning announcements changed into different letters right in front of my eyes.

CHAPTER TWO

I blinked a few times to make sure I wasn't hallucinating. What I'd just seen couldn't have been real.

At least the board had stopped shimmering, although instead of the morning announcements, it was full of information about the meanings of different colors. I glanced at the other students, and while a few of them smiled, they were mostly unfazed. They just watched me, waiting for me to say something. Darius also stood calmly, waiting for my reaction.

"How did you do that?" I finally asked.

"It's easy," Darius said. "I used magic. Well, a task like that wouldn't have been easy for you, since you're only in your second year of studies, but given enough practice you'll get the hang of it." He motioned to a seat in the second row, next to a girl with chin-length mousy brown hair. "Please sit down, and we'll resume class."

I stared at him, not moving. "You used ... magic," I repeated, the word getting stuck in my throat. I looked around the room again, waiting for someone to laugh. This had to be a joke. After all, an owl hadn't dropped a letter down my fireplace to let me know I'd been accepted into a special school, and I certainly hadn't taken an enchanted train to get to Kinsley High. "Funny. Now tell me what you *really* did."

"You mean you don't know?" Darius's forehead crinkled.

"Is this a special studies homeroom?" I asked. "And I somehow got put into one about ... magic tricks?"

"It wasn't a trick," said an athletic boy in the center of the room. His sandy hair fell below his ears, and he leaned back in his seat, pushing his sleeves up to his elbows. "Why use tricks when we can do the real thing?"

I stared at him blankly and backed towards the door. He couldn't be serious. Because magic—*real* magic—didn't exist. They must be playing a joke on me. Make fun of the new kid who hadn't grown up in a town so close to Salem.

I wouldn't fall for it. So I might as well play along.

"If that was magic, then where are your wands?" I held up a pretend wand, making a swooshing motion with my wrist.

Darius cleaned his glasses with the bottom of his

sweater. "I'd assumed you'd already started your lessons at your previous school." He frowned and placed his glasses back on. "From your reaction, I'm guessing that's not the case. I apologize for startling you. Unfortunately, there's no easy way to say this now, so I might as well be out with it." He took a deep breath, and said, "We're witches. You are, too. And regarding your question, we don't use wands because real witches don't need them. That's an urban legend created by humans who felt safer believing that they couldn't be harmed if there was no wand in sight."

"You can't be serious." I laughed nervously and pulled at the sleeves of my sweater. "Even if witches did exist—which they don't—I'm definitely not one of them."

The only thing "magical" that had ever happened to me was how the ligament I tore in my knee while playing tennis last month had healed right after moving here. The doctor had said it was a medical miracle.

But that didn't make it *magic*.

"I am completely serious," Darius said. "We're all witches, as are you. And this *is* a special studies homeroom—it's for the witches in the school. Although of course the administration doesn't know that." He chuckled. "They just think it's for highly gifted students. Now, please take a seat in the chair next to Kate, and I'll explain more."

I looked around the room, waiting for someone to end this joke. But the brown-haired girl who I assumed was Kate tucked her hair behind her ears and studied her hands. The athletic boy next to her watched me expectantly, and smiled when he caught me looking at him. A girl behind him glanced through her notes, and several other students shuffled in their seats.

My sweater felt suddenly constricting, and I swallowed away the urge to bolt out of there. This was a mistake, and I had to fix it. Now.

"I'm going to go back to the office to make sure they gave me the right schedule," I said, pointing my thumb at the door. "They must have put me in the wrong homeroom. But have fun talking about..." I looked at the board again to remind myself what it said. "Energy colors and their meanings."

They were completely out of their minds.

I hurried out of the classroom, feeling like I could breathe again once I was in the library lobby. No one else was around, and I sat in a chair to collect my thoughts. I would go back to the front office in a minute. For now, I browsed through my cell phone, wanting to see something familiar to remind myself that I wasn't going crazy.

Looking through my friends recent photos made me miss home even more. My eyes filled with tears at the thought of them living their lives without me. It hadn't been a week, and they'd already stopped texting me as often as usual. I was hundreds of miles away, and they were moving on, forgetting about me.

Not wanting anyone to see me crying, I wiped away the tears and switched my camera to front facing view to check my reflection. My eyes were slightly red, but not enough that anyone would notice. And my makeup was still intact.

I was about to put my phone away when I noticed something strange. The small scar above my left eyebrow—the one I'd gotten in fourth grade when I'd fallen on a playground—had disappeared. I brushed my index finger against the place where the indentation had been, expecting it to be a trick of the light. But the skin was soft and smooth.

As if the scar had never been there at all.

I dropped my hand down to my lap. Scars didn't disappear overnight, just like torn ligaments didn't repair themselves in days. And Darius had sounded so convinced that what he'd been saying was true. All of the students seemed to support what he was saying, too.

What if they actually believed what he was telling me? That magic *did* exist?

The thought was entertaining, but impossible. So I clicked out of the camera, put the phone back in my bag, and stood up. I had to get out of here. Maybe once I did, I would start thinking straight again.

"Nicole!" someone called from behind me. "Hold on a second."

I let out a long breath and turned around. The brown-haired girl Darius had called Kate was jogging in my direction. She was shorter than I'd originally thought, and the splattering of freckles across her nose made her look the same age as my younger sister Becca, who was in eighth grade. But that was where the similarities between Kate and Becca ended.

Because Kate was relatively plain looking, except for her eyes, which were a unique shade of bright, forest green.

"I know that sounded crazy in there," she said once she reached me. She picked at the side of her thumbnail, and while I suspected she wanted me to tell her that it didn't sound crazy, I couldn't lie like that.

"Yeah. It did." I shifted my feet, gripping the strap of my bag. "I know this is Massachusetts and witches are a part of the history here, so if you all believe in that stuff, that's fine. But it's not really my sort of thing."

"Keep your voice down." She scanned the area, but there was no one else in the library, so we were in the clear. "What Darius told you is real. How else would you explain what you saw in there, when he changed what was on the board?"

"A projector?" I shrugged. "Or maybe the board is a TV screen?"

"There's no projector." She held my gaze. "And the board isn't a television screen, even though that would be cool."

"Then I don't know." I glanced at the doors. "But magic wouldn't be on my list of explanations. No offense or anything."

"None taken," she said in complete seriousness. "But you were put in our homeroom for a reason. You're one of us. Think about it ... do strange things ever happen to you or people around you? Things that have no logical explanation?"

I opened my mouth, ready to say no, but closed it.

After all, two miraculous healings in a few days definitely counted as strange, although I wouldn't go so far as to call it *magic*.

But wasn't that the definition of a miracle— something that happened without any logical explanation, caused by something bigger than us? Something *magical*?

"It has." Kate smiled, bouncing on her toes. "Hasn't it?"

"I don't know." I shrugged, not wanting to tell her the specifics. It sounded crazy enough in my head— how would it sound when spoken out loud? "But I guess I'll go back with you for now. Only because the secretary said she won't adjust my schedule until the end of the day, anyway."

She smiled and led the way back to the classroom. Everyone stared at me again when we entered, and I didn't meet anyone's eyes as I took the empty chair next to her.

Darius nodded at us and waited for everyone to settle down. Once situated, I finally glanced around at the other students. The boy Darius had called Chris smiled at me, a girl with platinum hair filed her nails under the table, and the girl next to her looked like she was about to fall asleep. They were all typical high school students waiting for class to end.

But my eyes stopped at the end of the row on a guy with dark shaggy hair. His designer jeans and black leather jacket made him look like he'd come straight from a modeling shoot, and the casual way he leaned back in his chair exuded confidence and a carefree attitude. Then his gaze met mine, and goosebumps rose over my skin. His eyes were a startling shade of burnt brown, and they were soft, but calculating. Like he was trying to figure me out.

Kate rested an elbow on the table and leaned closer to me. "Don't even think about it," she whispered, and I yanked my gaze away from his, my cheeks flushing at the realization that I'd been caught staring at him. "That's Blake Carter. He's been dating Danielle Emerson since last year. She's the one to his left."

Not wanting to stare again, I glanced at Danielle from the corner of my eye. Her chestnut hair was supermodel thick, her ocean blue eyes were so bright that I wondered if they were colored contacts, and her black v-neck shirt dropped as low as possible without being overly inappropriate for school.

Of course Blake had a girlfriend, and she was beautiful. I never stood a chance.

"As I said earlier, we're going to review the energy colors and what they mean," Darius said, interrupting my thoughts. "But before we begin, who can explain to Nicole how we use energy?"

I sunk down in my seat, hating that the attention had been brought back to me. Luckily, the athletic boy next to Kate who'd said the thing earlier about magic not being a trick raised his hand.

"Chris," Darius called on him. "Go ahead."

Chris pushed his hair off his forehead and faced me. His t-shirt featured an angry storm cloud holding a lighting bolt like a baseball bat, with "Trenton Thunder" written below it. It was goofy, and not a sports team that I'd ever heard of. But his boyish grin and rounded cheeks made him attractive in a cute way. Not in the same "stop what you're doing because I'm walking in your direction" way as Blake, but he definitely would have gotten attention from the girls at my old school.

"There's energy everywhere." Chris moved his hands in a giant arc above his head to demonstrate. "Humans know that energy exists—they've harnessed it for electronics. The difference between us and humans is that we have the power to tap into energy and use it ourselves, and humans don't." He smiled at me, as if I was supposed to understand what he meant. "Make sense?"

"Not really," I said. "Sorry."

"It's easier if you relate it to something familiar," he said, speaking faster. "What happens to the handle of a metal spoon when you leave it in boiling water?"

"It gets hot?" I said it as a question. This was stuff people learned in fifth grade science—not high school homeroom.

"And what happens when it's plastic?"

"It doesn't get hot," I said slowly. "It stays room temperature."

"Exactly." He grinned at me like I'd just solved an astrophysics mathematical equation. "Humans are like plastic. Even if they're immersed in energy, they can't conduct it. Witches are like metal. We have the ability to absorb energy and control it as we want."

"So, how do we take in this energy?" I asked, since I might as well humor him.

"Through our hands." Chris turned his palms up, closed his eyes, and took a deep breath. He looked like a meditating Buddha. Students snickered, and Chris re-opened his eyes, pushed his sleeves up, and sat back in his chair.

"O-o-kay." I elongated the word, smiling and laughing along with everyone else.

Darius cleared his throat, and everyone calmed down. "We can conduct energy from the Universe into our bodies," he said, his voice full of authority. Chills passed through me, and even though I still didn't believe any of this, I sat back to listen. "Once we've harnessed it, we can use it as we like. Think of energy like light. It contains different colors, each relating to an aspect of life. I've written them on the board. The most basic exercise we learn in this class is to sense this energy and absorb it. Just open your mind, envision the color you're focusing on, and picture it entering your body through your palms."

I rotated my hand to look at my palm. It looked normal—not like it was about to open up and absorb energy from the Universe.

"We're going to do a meditation session," Darius continued. "Everyone should pick a color from the board and picture it as energy entering your palms. Keep it simple and absorb the energy—don't push it back out into the Universe. This exercise is for practice and self-improvement." He looked at me, a hint of challenge in his eyes. "Now, please pick a color and begin."

I looked around the room to see what others were

doing. Most people already had their eyes closed, the muscles in their faces calm and relaxed. They were really getting into this. As if they truly believed it.

If I didn't at least *look* like I was trying, I would stand out—again. So I might as well go along with it and pretend.

I re-examined the board and skimmed through the "meanings" of the colors. Red caught my attention first. It apparently increased confidence, courage, and love, along with attraction and desire. The prospect made me glance at Blake, who sat still with his eyes closed, his lips set in a line of concentration.

But he was out of my league *and* he had a girlfriend. I shouldn't waste my time hoping for anything to happen between us.

Instead, I read through the other colors and settled on green. It supposedly brought growth, success, and luck, along with helping a person open their mind, become more aware of options, and choose a good path. Those were all things I needed right now.

I opened my palms towards the ceiling and closed my eyes. Once comfortable, I steadied my breathing and tried clearing my mind.

Then there was the question of how to "channel" a color. Picturing it seemed like a good start, so I imagined myself pulling green out of the air, the color glowing with life. A soft hum filled my ears as it expanded and pushed against me, like waves crashing over my skin. The palms of my hands tingled, and the energy flowed through my body, joining with my blood as it pumped through my veins. It streamed up my arms, moved down to my stomach, and poured down to my toes. Green glowed behind my eyelids, and I kept gathering it and gathering it until it grew so much that it had nowhere else to go.

Then it pushed its way out of my palms with such force that it must have lit up the entire room.

CHAPTER THREE

The bell rang, and my eyes snapped open, the classroom coming into focus. I looked around, taking in the scuffed tiled floor, the chalkboard covered with writing, the white plaster walls, and the lack of windows. Everything looked normal. Unchanged. There was no proof that anything I'd just felt had been more than a figment of my imagination.

But that energy flowing through my body had been so *real*. I tightened my hands into fists and opened them back up, but only a soft tingle remained. Then it disappeared completely.

Kate stood up, dropped her backpack on her chair, and studied me. "I'm guessing from the look on your face that it worked," she said.

"I don't know." I shrugged and picked up my bag. "I'm not sure what was supposed to happen." I met her eyes and managed a small smile, since it wasn't exactly a lie.

But the energy I'd felt around me was unlike anything I'd ever experienced. Which meant my imagination was running out of control. Because there was no proof that I'd done anything. What I'd "experienced" had existed only in my head. Right?

Kate glanced at her watch. "What class do you have first?"

I pulled out my schedule. "Honors Biology." I scrunched my nose at the prospect. "They put me in all honors classes, and I have no idea why. I was in regular classes at my old school."

"I've got Honors Bio, too," she said. "Come on. I'll explain the whole honors thing on the way there."

I followed Kate down the hallway, although I kept bumping into people, since my mind was spinning after what had happened in homeroom. I'd felt something during that meditation session. Maybe it was the energy that Darius was talking about. And if this energy stuff *was* the reason behind the miraculous recovery of my torn tendon and the healed scar ...

I pushed the thought away. There had to be another explanation. One that made *sense*.

Kate edged closer to the wall to give me space to walk next to her. "So, about the honors classes," she said, lowering her voice. "You saw what was written on the board. Each color has a different meaning. Once we learn how to harness energy properly, we can use the different colors to help us ... do things."

"What kind of things?" I asked.

"Let's take yellow—my personal favorite—as an example," she said. "Yellow increases focus and helps us remember information. If you channel yellow energy before studying for a test, it won't take as long to review everything, and you'll remember more. It'll make your memory almost photographic. Pretty cool, right?"

"It does sound useful," I agreed. "Although I'm still not buying all this colors and energy stuff."

"Give it time." Kate smiled, as if she knew something I didn't, and stopped in front of a classroom door. "We're here. Want to sit with me?" She led the way to a table in the front, and I followed, even though front and center wasn't my thing. "I'll help you with the basics after school," she offered. "You got the hang of channeling energy pretty quickly, so it shouldn't be hard. Sometimes it takes the freshmen months to gather enough energy to feel anything significant. It was obvious from where I was sitting that you did it on your first try. That was pretty impressive."

"I'm not sure I actually did anything, but sure, I'll study with you after school," I said. Even though this energy stuff sounded crazy, it was nice of Kate to reach out. I didn't want to miss the chance to make my first friend here. "I could definitely use help getting caught up with my classes."

"Great." Kate beamed. "I'm sure you'll pick it up quickly."

More students piled in, a few of them people I recognized from homeroom. Then, just as I'd started to think it was stupid to hope he would also be in this class, Blake strolled inside, with Danielle trailing close behind.

His eyes met mine, and my breath caught, taken aback by how he'd noticed me again. But he couldn't be interested in me like *that*. It was probably just because I was new. And because, as embarrassing as it was to admit, he'd caught me staring at him. So I opened my textbook to the chapter that Kate already had open, focusing on a section on dominant and recessive genes as if it were the most fascinating thing I'd ever read in my life.

"I told you in homeroom that he's taken, remember?" Kate whispered once Blake and Danielle were far enough away.

My cheeks heated. "Was it that obvious?"

"That you were checking him out?" Kate asked, and I nodded, despite how humiliating it was that she'd noticed. "Yeah."

"I'm not doing it on purpose," I said. "I know that he has a girlfriend. I would never try anything, I promise. But ... have you seen him? It was hard not to at least *look*."

"I know you're not doing it on purpose," she said. "He's one of the hottest guys in the school—I get that. But Danielle doesn't take it too kindly when girls flirt with Blake. Or check out Blake. Or even look like they're *interested* in Blake. It's in your best interest to keep your distance from both of them. Trust me."

I was about to ask why, but before I could, the bell rang and class began.

CHAPTER FOUR

The other sophomores from homeroom were in most of my classes, and Kate sat with me in each one, including lunch. I was so behind in the honors courses that I seriously needed whatever Kate said she would teach me after school to help.

"What class do you have next?" Kate asked as we packed our bags after advanced Spanish.

I pulled my schedule out of my pocket. "Ceramics." I groaned. I wasn't awful at art, but I would have preferred a music elective, since music was always my favorite class. "What about you?"

"Theatre," she answered, tucking her hair behind her ears. "I want to be in the school play this spring, but I always get nervous on stage. Hopefully the class will help."

"You'll get in," I said. "Besides, can't you use that witchy energy stuff to convince the teacher to give you the part you want? Or mess up other people during their auditions so they don't get the leads?"

Her eyes darted around the hall, and she leaned in closer, lowering her voice. "We don't use our powers to take advantage of others," she said. "I'll fill you in on everything later. Okay?"

I nodded and followed her through the art wing, resisting the urge to ask her more right now. Instead, I looked around. Student paintings decorated the walls, and what sounded like a flute solo came from a room close by. Kate stopped in front of the double doors that led to the theatre. "This is me," she said. "The ceramics room is upstairs—you shouldn't miss it."

We split ways, and like Kate had told me, the ceramics room was easy to find. Kilns lined the side wall, pottery wheels were on the other end, bricks of clay were stacked in shelves in the back, and the huge windows were a welcome change from the stuffy classrooms I'd been in so far.

I looked around to see if anyone seemed receptive to having the new girl join them, and my eyes stopped when they reached Blake's. He sat at the table furthest away, leaning back in his seat with his legs outstretched. The chairs next to him were empty. He nodded at me, as if acknowledging me as a member of a special club, and I noticed that no one else from homeroom was in this class. Could he be inviting me to sit with him?

Since everyone from homeroom seemed to stick together, I took that as a yes and walked toward Blake's table, my pulse quickening with every step. I remembered what Kate had told me earlier about Danielle—how she was crazy possessive over Blake—but Danielle wasn't here. And Blake was the only person who wanted me to join him. Refusing would be rude.

He moved his legs to give me room, and I settled in the seat next to him. His deep, liquid eyes had various shades of reddish brown running through them, and he was watching me as if he was waiting for me to say something. I swallowed, not sure how to start, and settled on the obvious.

"Hi." My heart pounded so hard I feared he could hear it. "You're in my homeroom, right?"

"Yep," he said smoothly. "We also have biology, history, and Spanish together." He counted off each on his fingers. "And given that you're in Darius's homeroom, it's safe to say that you have Greek mythology with me next period as well. I'm Blake."

"Nicole," I introduced myself, even though Darius had already done so in front of the class this morning. "I heard that all of the sophomores in our homeroom have to take Greek mythology. Luckily I read *The Odyssey* in English last year, so I shouldn't be totally lost."

"There's a reason we're required to take Greek mythology." He scooted closer to me, as if about to tell me a secret, and I leaned forward in anticipation. "Did you know that we—meaning everyone in our homeroom—are descended from the Greek gods?"

I arched an eyebrow. "Like Zeus and all of them living in a castle on the clouds?" I asked.

"Exactly." He smirked. "Except that they're referred to as the Olympians, and they call their 'castle in the clouds' Mount Olympus."

"So you're saying that we're *gods*?"

"We're not gods." He smiled and shook his head. "But we have 'diluted god blood' in us. It's what gives us our powers."

"Right." I wasn't sure how else to respond, and I looked down at the table. Was he playing a joke on me? Trying to see how gullible the new kid could be?

"What's wrong?" He watched me so intensely—so seriously—that I knew he was truly concerned.

"The truth?" I asked, and he nodded, his gaze locked on mine. So I took a deep breath, and said, "Everything from our homeroom sounds crazy to me. But you're all so serious about it that I'm starting to think you actually believe it."

"It's a lot to take in at once," he said.

"That's the understatement of the day." I flaked a piece of dried clay off the table with my thumbnail. "But Kate offered to teach me some stuff after school, and she's been really nice by taking me around all day, so I told her I would listen to her."

"Kate's a rule follower," Blake said, crossing his arms. "She's only going to tell you about a fraction of the stuff we can do. But stay in homeroom with us, and maybe my friends and I will show you how to have *real* fun with our abilities."

The teacher walked inside before I could respond, and the chattering in the room quieted. As much as I wanted to ask Blake what he meant, I couldn't right now. We weren't supposed to talk about our abilities when humans could hear.

Then I realized: I'd thought of other people as "humans," like I wasn't one of them anymore.

The scary thing was—I might be starting to believe it.

CHAPTER FIVE

After Greek mythology, Kate and I walked together to the classroom in the library. Darius was there, hunched over his desk as he studied a paper. Kate knocked on the door, and Darius flinched backward, lifting his head to look at us.

"Nicole." He picked up the paper and put it into his briefcase. "I'm glad you're back. I wanted to apologize again for the dramatic way I introduced all of this to you this morning. I didn't realize that you were coming in here knowing nothing."

"It was certainly dramatic." I looked at the board where the writing had changed in front of my eyes that morning. "And to be honest, I'm still not sure if I believe any of it. It seems very..." I paused, not wanting to say anything that he might take as insulting.

"Far-fetched?" he completed my thought, and I nodded. "I wouldn't blame you for thinking that. However, what's your instinct telling you?"

"My instinct can't get over how witches are creatures from fairy tales—or horror stories," I said. "They don't exist."

"Give it time." He waved my answer away, and packed up his stuff. "I shouldn't have asked you so soon."

"Hold on," I said, since I still wanted answers. "What did you do to the board this morning? When you made the letters move?"

"I didn't 'make the letters move.'" He chuckled. "Our powers are mental, not physical. So before you came inside, I created an illusion to hide what was *really* written on the board. Once I determined your identity, I removed the illusion to allow you to see what it actually said."

"You 'created an illusion,'" I repeated, shaking my head. "I guess I shouldn't have expected something that made sense."

"It *will* make sense," he said. "Just give it time. After all, you did a fantastic job with harnessing energy this morning during our practice session. You chose green, did you not?"

"I did," I said, gripping the strap of my bag. "How did you know that?"

"I felt it fill the room," he said. "It was impossible *not* to sense it. Well, at least impossible for me. None of the other students are advanced enough to have been able to tell. But that was quite impressive, especially for a first try. It would be a shame to waste such natural talent."

I stood there, unsure what to say. I hadn't told *anyone* what color I'd chosen that morning. How could Darius have known?

It was either an excellent guess, or he was telling the truth.

"I'm going to go over the basics with Nicole," Kate spoke up. "I want to help catch her up."

"Thank you, Kate," Darius said. "I know you'll lead her in the right direction. In the meantime, I'm going to get out of your way. I'll see both of you tomorrow morning."

"Bye." I made no promises about being in his homeroom tomorrow, since I was still considering changing my schedule. "Thanks for letting us use the room."

"This room is yours as much as it is mine," he said as he walked to the door. "Good luck, and have fun."

"We will," Kate said, and he shut the door, leaving us on our own. Once he was gone, Kate clasped her hands together, her eyes shining. "What do you want to learn first?" she asked.

"You're the expert," I said. "But the whole 'making studying take less time than normal' thing might be a good place to start. I'm way behind in Spanish."

"Good idea," she agreed. "How about we do some focus and memorization exercises? It's one of the first things freshmen do when they learn how to harness energy. Darius should have something to practice with. Hold on a minute while I look." She walked to the row of cabinets on the side of the room and pulled out a box. "Here it is."

"Is that Trivial Pursuit?" I chuckled at the sight of the game that I used to love back when my family did weekly game nights.

"It helps with memorization," she said. "Like flashcards. And you learn a bunch of fun facts as well." She set the box down and opened it. "So, you really didn't know about *any* of this before this morning?"

"No..." I said. "I thought that was obvious by now."

"It is," she said. "It's just surprising that your parents didn't tell you. Even without training, your powers would show themselves eventually. You would think they would have wanted to prepare you."

"They don't know about any of this," I said. "So they couldn't have known to tell me."

"That's not possible." Kate's eyes lit up at the opportunity to share her knowledge. "Since we're all descended from the Greek gods, our powers are passed down from one generation to the next. A witch has to have one parent who's also a witch."

"I guess it was my bio-dad," I said bitterly, finishing setting up the game by plopping the last pile of cards where it belonged.

"Oh." Kate shifted in her seat and straightened the piles of cards, not meeting my eyes. I suspected she wanted to ask what I meant, but that she didn't want to make me feel uncomfortable.

"My bio-dad left before I was born." My throat tightened, and I swallowed to make the lump go away. I barely talked about this—let alone with someone I'd just met. But Kate seemed to genuinely want to help, and she couldn't do that if I wasn't honest with her. "My mom hasn't heard from him since. But she married my step-dad a few months later, and he's my dad in every way but biologically."

"Wow." Kate picked at her nails. "I'm sorry."

"It's fine," I said. "I barely think about my bio-dad. Like I said, my step-dad is my dad. But from what you told me so far ... it sounds like my bio-dad might have been a witch, and never mentioned it to my mom." I laughed at how ridiculous it sounded. "That is, *if* any of this is true. I'm still unsure about it."

"Well, you've gone from being positive it's not real to being 'unsure,'" Kate said. "So that's a start. But you're allowed to talk to your family about it. Immediate family members without abilities are the only humans allowed to know about what we can do."

"I can't tell them," I said. "Because even if this is real, I have no proof. Without proof, my mom and dad will think I've lost my mind, and my sister will make fun of me forever. Or she would be jealous that I have powers and she doesn't."

"I know what you mean." Kate laughed. "My brother's in seventh grade, and he hates that I'm allowed to use my powers and he isn't. He's already started a countdown for how many days he has left until high school."

"He's not allowed to use his powers until high

school?" I asked.

"None of us are," Kate said. "The Elders don't want kids messing around with abilities they don't understand yet."

"But what's to stop him from using his powers, anyway?"

"The same thing that stops us from driving a car before we're sixteen," she said. "It's the law. If a witch is caught using powers underage, the Head Elders—the most powerful witches in the world, who enforce our laws—block their powers so they have to wait a year until they can start learning. If they're caught twice they have to wait two years, and so on."

"So why don't the Head Elders block everyone's powers until high school?" I asked.

"That would make sense, wouldn't it?" Kate said. "But they wouldn't do that, because our powers aren't developed enough at that age to cause any harm, and the Elders are testing us to see if we follow the rules. Of course, some people use their powers underage and don't get caught, but I never thought it was worth the risk."

"But other people did," I said, leaning forward. "Does Danielle happen to be one of them?"

"You catch on quick." Kate smiled. "She does. And of course she didn't get caught."

"So that's why you don't like her?"

"Not exactly." Kate's eyes darted around the room, as if she were worried someone was listening. "There are some of our kind who don't like humans—mainly the ones from pure-blood witch families—and Danielle is one of them. She sees humans as a lesser species. She doesn't care if she hurts them or not."

"What does she do?" I rested my arm on the table, way more interested in gossiping than studying.

"Nothing that's been confirmed." Kate chewed on her lower lip and pushed her hair behind her ears. "But last semester I heard a rumor that she caught a junior girl flirting with Blake at a party, so she used gray energy to make the girl disoriented before she drove home."

"I didn't see gray energy on the board this morning," I said. "What does it do?"

"Most of the energy colors are positive, but gray energy makes people disoriented and confused," she said. "It wasn't on the board because we're not encouraged to use it. Gray energy is the second worst one to pure black energy, which is extremely difficult—and illegal—to use."

"Wow," I said. "That sounds dangerous."

"It is," Kate agreed. "Which is why we're not taught how to use it. Only the strongest witches can access black energy, and if the Elders find out that someone's using it, that person risks having their powers purged completely."

"So the Elders can take powers away?" I asked. "Permanently?"

"Yes," Kate said. "It's the most excruciating experience one of our kind can go through, and it's a punishment for only the worst crimes. Danielle's not strong enough to use black energy, but I wouldn't be surprised if she knew the basics of using gray. Gray energy is frowned upon, but not illegal, and we all suspect that Danielle and her friends study it in private."

I nodded, remembering what Blake had said to me in ceramics—about how if I spent time with him and his friends, I could learn better ways to use my powers. Was this what he'd been talking about? Did he, Danielle, and their friends secretly practice using gray energy?

"So, the girl who Danielle made disoriented before she drove home," I said, returning to the earlier conversation. "She's okay, right?"

"Barely," Kate said, her expression grim. "She lost control of the car and hit a tree. She was in a coma for two weeks, and the doctors weren't sure if she was going to make it. Luckily she woke up, but she had brain damage, so she's home schooled now. She might never get back to the way she was before the accident. And there's no way to prove that Danielle did anything."

I sat back in my chair and breathed out slowly. "That's awful," I said. "Danielle didn't strike me as a particularly nice person, but that just sounds ... evil."

"Yeah," Kate agreed. "Which is why you shouldn't get on Danielle's bad side—especially when it comes to Blake."

"If she's that jealous, maybe she should worry more about her relationship with Blake than the girls he talks to," I said.

"I agree," Kate said. "But I still think it's best to keep your distance."

"Right," I said, even though I had a feeling that I wouldn't be able to resist sitting next to him in ceramics again. "But if Danielle does something like that again ... couldn't we take her on if we wanted? Do something to stop her?"

"That's a strong statement from someone who claims not to believe in any of this." Kate laughed, although it came out as an awkward squeaky sound. "In order to 'take someone on,' you have to know what you're doing. And you're just getting started. So, what do you say that we get back to the basics?"

"Yes." I nodded and sat straighter. "I'm ready."

"First you need to learn how our control over energy works," Kate said. "We can absorb it from the Universe, and then throw it back out to the Universe to create change. But we can't put out more energy than we take in, and absorbing energy requires us to use energy. You'll know when your body needs to stop—you'll start feeling weak and tired—and you have to listen to it."

"I don't understand." I frowned. "I thought energy is endless."

"It is." She nodded. "But our bodies can only do so much. Think about it like a battery. We need time to recharge."

"And what if we use up more energy than we have?"

"You'll fry out your battery," she said. "You'll die. Energy is our life force. Without it, we can't survive. But barely anyone has ever gotten to that point, because if you got close, you would feel so exhausted that you would *want* to stop. You would probably collapse before you would be able to deplete your energy and fry out."

"So we only have a certain amount of energy, and we can use it to conduct the energy around us," I said, wanting to make sure I was getting this straight. She nodded, and I continued, "You said that humans can't conduct energy. But if there's energy in everything, then they have some in them too, right?"

"Yeah." Kate picked at her nails and looked down at the table.

"So if they can't use it, is there any way that we can ... borrow it so we can have more of our own? As long as we don't take enough to kill them?"

"Technically we can," she said, lowering her voice. "But taking someone else's energy is illegal. If the Head Elders find out, the punishment is death. You see, once a witch takes someone else's energy—from a human or another witch—their body stops producing energy on its own. They become leeches, dependent on the energy of others forever. And once a witch starts taking someone's energy, it's so consuming that it's nearly impossible for them to stop until they've taken it all."

"You mean they end up killing the person?" I drew back in my seat, my eyes wide. "Like a vampire—but by draining energy instead of blood?"

"Vampires don't exist, but that's where the legends come from," Kate said, her expression grave.

"How many of them are out there?" I asked.

"Not many," she said. "The few who are out there live in hiding, and the Elders hunt them down and ...

take care of them. Anyway," she said, "They're rare—they're more urban legends than anything else. And we still have so much to cover today. Are you ready to continue?"

"Yes," I said, feeling more determined now than ever. "Let's do this."

CHAPTER SIX

Kate drove me home after the study session, and soon enough she was pulling into my driveway. The house still didn't feel like mine. The gray wood panels, thatched roof, and blue shutters reminded me of a grandmother's cottage. I missed my bright, sprawling house in Georgia. Every time I saw this house, I was reminded about how different it was from what I left behind.

"Thanks for showing me around today and helping me out after school," I told her as I hopped out of the car. "And for driving me home."

"Any time," she replied. "I'll see you in homeroom tomorrow."

She backed out of the driveway, waving again

before she turned around the corner.

I hurried down the sidewalk and up the steps to the porch. The freezing air numbed my body to the bones, and I pulled my jacket tighter around me. I was never going to get used to this weather. People were not supposed to live in places as cold as the arctic tundra.

Silence greeted me when I stepped inside. Becca was probably in her room messaging her friends, and my dad didn't get off work until later that evening. My mom was most likely painting, so I walked up the back steps to the "bonus room" above the garage that she'd turned into an art studio. Music echoed through the hall, confirming my suspicions that she was painting. She normally wasn't thrilled to get interrupted while working, but since it was my first day at a new school, she would want to hear about how it went.

I also had to somehow figure out if she knew about my bio-dad being a witch—without telling her about what I'd learned today.

I opened the door, and paint fumes filled my nose, making my eyes water. Just as I'd expected, my mom was hard at work, her back towards me, her hair pulled up in a messy ponytail. A few splatters of paint had already landed on the cloth beneath the easel.

"Hey, Mom," I said, knocking on the open door.

She swiveled around on her stool, and a glob of paint fell to the ground. "Hey," she greeted me, waving the paintbrush in the air. The freckles splattered over the bridge of her nose made her look younger than she was, and in her baggy green t-shirt from an old Clash concert, she looked like she could still be in her twenties. "How was your first day?"

"It was fine." My throat tightened at the lie, and I swallowed, trying to relax. I would tell her the truth— eventually. "There were a few people I met who showed me around."

"That's good." She smiled and placed the paintbrush down. "Any cute guys?"

"Maybe." I rolled my eyes. Of course that would be one of her first questions. "But he has a girlfriend, so it doesn't matter."

"You're still in high school." She laughed and pushed some wisps of hair off her face, getting a smudge of blue paint on her forehead. "As long as he's not married, he's on the market."

"It seems like they're pretty serious." I tried to keep my tone light. "Besides, the school's big. He's not the only guy there."

"But he's the only one who caught your eye?"

"I guess." I shrugged. My cheeks heated at the thought of Blake, remembering the intense way he'd looked at me during our short conversation in ceramics, and I focused on the ground.

"You should go for him." Her voice softened, and her eyes went distant. "You don't want to look back and regret not knowing what might have happened."

I sat down on the wooden chair next to her and took a deep breath. "You're talking about *him*, aren't you?" I asked. "Aidan?"

I didn't usually say my bio-dad's name out loud, but after my discussion with Kate, I had to. I needed to know more about him.

ELEMENTALS

"Yes." She nodded and studied the painting she'd been working on. It was only halfway done, but once finished, it would look perfect with the vibrant, abstract pieces in her collection.

"What was he like?" I asked, not for the first time.

"He was charming," she said, her eyes sad. "And he was very handsome—like an ancient statue brought to life. You look so much like him." Her eyes watered, and I knew I should stop now.

But I tightened my grip on the edge of the chair and asked, "How did you two meet?"

She picked up her paintbrush again and pushed an imaginary strand of hair behind her ear. "Why are you bringing this up now?" she asked. "He's in our past. You've never asked me this much about him before."

"We're studying genetics in bio," I said the first excuse that came to my mind. "It got me thinking ... he's my biological father. I should know more about him."

"Like if his earlobes are connected and if he can roll his tongue?" she teased, although her lower lip trembled. She looked away from me to study her painting. I knew she wanted me to tell her never mind—that I didn't have to know that badly—but I didn't budge. After what I'd learned today, I had to know more.

"I barely know *anything* about him—not even how you met," I said. "Isn't that something I should know?"

"You're right." She blinked a few times and took a deep breath, clasping her hands in her lap. "I suppose it would have been a great story, if it had ended well,"

45

she said, her voice surprisingly steady. "You see, in the spring production during my senior year in college, I played the part of Christine in Phantom of the Opera. The lead role. He—Aidan—attended our last show. He was so impressed with my performance that he waited outside of the stage door for over an hour to talk with me." She smiled, her eyes distant and full of light, as if she were re-living the moment. "We ended up talking until the sun rose. It was a perfect night. For the next two months, we were inseparable."

"Did he ever do anything ... different?" I asked. "Anything special?"

"He was the most impressive man I'd ever met," she said. "He was so talented—it was like every instrument he picked up he could play perfectly. I couldn't believe that he'd noticed me. I felt so average next to him, but during those few weeks when we were together, it was like living in a dream. Then I found out I was pregnant with you."

I knew I hadn't been planned, but I wrapped my arms around myself, guilt filling my chest at how I'd ruined my mom's happiness with Aidan.

"It was unexpected, but I was looking forward to the three of us being a family." She picked up a clean paintbrush, running her finger across the bristles. "I told Aidan about you, and he said he was happy, but the next day he just ... disappeared. I hated him for abandoning us. But my parents helped me through it, and I moved back home after graduation and reconnected with Jerry—you know we dated in high school—and he helped me find happiness again. He promised he would love you as if you were his own, and he's done that every day. So yes, there are times when I wonder how Aidan could leave us like that, but if it hadn't been for him, I wouldn't have had you. So for that, I'm grateful."

"Aidan just ... left?" I swallowed, my voice cracking. "So easily? Have you heard from him since?"

I knew the answer, but I needed to hear her say it out loud.

"No." She shook her head and turned back to her painting. "It's like he fell off the planet."

I nodded, knowing I shouldn't have hoped for anything else. If Aidan had wanted to be in our lives, he would have reached out to us. But he never had. He probably never would. The reminder of that hard truth stung every time.

"Anyway, your dad's going to be home soon," Mom said. "How about we check out that restaurant near the cove for dinner? It's supposed to be beautiful— floor to ceiling windows looking out over the water."

With that, the conversation was over, and I headed to my room to get ready for dinner.

I hadn't gotten the information I was hoping for, but I had a gut feeling that Aidan *had* to be a witch. It could be why he'd left. And now I was more determined than ever—I was going to get answers.

If that meant staying in Darius's homeroom, then so be it.

CHAPTER SEVEN

Darius strolled into homeroom the next morning wearing another brown tweed suit. "Good morning," he said, smiling when he saw that I was still there. "We have a lot to cover today, so let's jump straight to it. Who can tell us about the event happening tomorrow night?"

"Tomorrow's the night of the Olympian Comet," Blake answered smoothly, not bothering to raise his hand. "It's coming around for the first time in three thousand years."

"Correct." Darius said. "And who can explain the importance of the Olympian Comet?"

"The comet is very powerful." Danielle also hadn't bothered raising her hand, and she flipped her hair over her shoulder. "The Olympians used its power to lock up the Titans and banish them from the Earth."

"Thank you, Danielle." Darius gave her a small nod. "But let's backtrack. Why did the Olympians want to lock up the Titans to begin with?"

Kate's hand shot into the air.

"Kate?" Darius lifted his chin and smiled, like he knew whatever she said would be correct.

"The Olympians are the children of the Titans," Kate said, like she was reciting the answer from a textbook. "The fight between the Olympians and the Titans started after a prophecy that said that Cronus—the leader of the Titans—would be overthrown by his kids. In order to prevent this prophecy from happening, Cronus ate each one of his children after they were born. His wife eventually had enough of him eating their kids, so she rescued the youngest one—Zeus—by having Cronus eat a rock instead. She brought up Zeus in a secret cave. Once Zeus grew up he freed his brothers and sisters, who were still alive inside of Cronus's stomach, and they all rebelled against Cronus, overthrowing him and his supporters in the Battle of the Titans. Then Zeus locked the Titans down in Tartarus—the deepest pit in Hades' underworld—where he hoped they would stay for good."

"Good job, Kate," Darius said, and she sat straighter, clearly pleased with herself. "But the Titans didn't give up that easily. What did they do in retaliation?"

"The Olympians retreated to their home on Mount Olympus, and the Titans used their time in Tartarus to plan the Second Rebellion," Blake answered before anyone could raise a hand. "Cronus's servant discovered a portal to escape Tartarus, and the Titans prepared for a battle to regain their place as rulers. They caught the Olympians by surprise, and they nearly won. But then a powerful comet shot through the sky, and the Olympians used the magic from the comet to gather enough energy to defeat the Titans once more. That's why it's named the Olympian Comet. This time the Olympians locked the Titans up in Kerberos—a shadow world that's impossible to escape. They spent centuries banishing all of the Titans' supporters—demons, monsters, and other evil creatures—to Kerberos as well, before sealing the portal and returning to Mount Olympus."

"Correct," Darius said.

For someone who'd been acting like this was all a myth yesterday, Blake sure knew this story well. But there was one big part that didn't make sense.

"If this is all true, why does no one believe in the Olympians anymore?" I didn't raise my hand, since speaking out of turn seemed to be protocol around here. "If the Olympians are real, why don't they show themselves and set everyone straight?"

Some people in the back whispered, and Darius held his hands up for them to be quiet.

"The Ancient Greeks used to worship the gods," Darius explained, pacing in the front of the room. "Then the Romans adopted the religion, making it their own by renaming the gods and giving them traits that better suited their society. But the essence of their belief was the same. Then, their beliefs changed. Does anyone want to tell us why?"

A blonde girl spoke up from the back of the room. "Constantine instated Christianity in Rome as an official religion around 300 CE," she said softly. "The Romans swayed to Christianity, and monotheism overtook the Western world. But people continued to practice the ancient beliefs in secret, and Dodekatheism—the revival of ancient Greek religious practices—publicly re-emerged at the turn of the twentieth century. Our numbers might be small, but they do exist."

"Thank you, Jessica," Darius said with a smile. "And to answer your second question, Nicole, the gods do occasionally journey to Earth, although it's usually in disguise. In fact, it was Ares himself, the god of war, who was behind the assassination of the Archduke Franz Ferdinand of Austria. As some of you may know from history classes, this assassination started World War I. Ares loves battles and slaughter, so creating that kind of turmoil is entertaining to him."

I nodded, even though I hadn't taken European history yet and didn't know much about World War I. "So the gods sometimes come down to Earth in disguise," I repeated, trying to take this all in. "But what about all of the other ... creatures? The ones from the stories who didn't support the Titans in the Second Rebellion and who weren't locked in Kerberos? What happened to them?"

"The harmless ones still live among us, although they create illusions to hide their true forms," Darius said. "They don't want to risk humans killing them with technology or using them in experiments. Then there are some dangerous creatures who aren't in Kerberos because they didn't support the Titans in the Second Rebellion. They're also aware that human technology is a threat, so they keep a low profile. The Elders take care of any problems they create."

I nodded, since I had a feeling that "taking care" of them meant killing them.

"More present-day references to the Greek gods exist than you realize," Darius continued. "Chris's shoes are a prime example."

I glanced at Chris's sneakers, which looked like they came straight from the eighties—white with the blue Nike swoosh mark on the side. I had a similar pair in pink.

"Sneakers are from the Greek gods?" I asked. "I always thought the Greeks wore leather sandals."

"Not sneakers." Darius chuckled. "I'm referring to the brand. Nike."

I frowned, because of course I'd heard of Nike. My town in Georgia might be small compared to Kinsley, but I wasn't from another planet. "How does Nike relate to the gods?" I asked.

"Nike is the Greek goddess of victory, speed, and strength." He counted off each trait on his fingers. "Does the Nike swoosh remind you of anything else?"

"Isn't it a checkmark?"

"Look closer," he said. "What else do you see?"

I squinted and tilted my head to view it from a different angle. "Nothing else," I said. "Only the checkmark."

"As most people do." He took off his glasses and cleaned the lenses with his sweater. "But the goddess Nike is also known as the Winged Goddess of Victory. The swoosh is the shape of a wing."

"Hmm." I studied Chris's shoes. "Now that you say it, I do kind of see it."

Darius smiled, then refocused on the class. "As I mentioned before break, we're going to view the comet together tomorrow night." He picked up a piece of chalk and wrote on the board. "This is my address, and I expect you all to be there by 9:00 PM. This event should be viewed as a mandatory 'field trip.' Anyone who doesn't show up without a written excuse from a parent will have detention for a month."

The bell rang, and I wrote down the address.

After all, the last thing I needed on my first week at a new school was detention.

CHAPTER EIGHT

Darius lived on Odessa Road, the main street through town. Kate and I arrived at his house about five minutes before nine o'clock. Wind whipped through the air as we walked down the sidewalk, and I wrapped my arms around myself, trying to ignore the numbing cold.

Darius's log cabin didn't fit in with the typical New England homes in the area. Trees surrounded it on all sides, and if I didn't know any better, I would have thought it was the only house around for miles.

Hearing chattering from outside, Kate and I followed the sidewalk to the backyard. It was big enough to fit everyone from our homeroom. No clouds blocked the stars, making it a perfect night to watch the comet.

The only thing not perfect was the temperature. Even though Kate told me that it was warmer than a usual January night in Massachusetts, my blood still felt like it would turn to ice if I stood in one place for too long. Hopefully the leggings underneath my jeans, the black sheepskin boots that reached my knees, and puffy jacket would be enough protection from the biting cold.

People were gathered on the deck, around a steel container for drinks, and I walked over to grab one. Hot chocolate came out of the small faucet. I blew on it to cool it down, enjoying the tingling warmth of steam on my cheeks.

"Are you excited for the comet?" someone asked over my shoulder. I jumped, splattering a few drops of hot chocolate on the deck, and turned to find Chris. I hadn't noticed his eyes before, but now, under the glow of the moon, they appeared almost yellow.

"It should be interesting," I said, taking a sip of hot chocolate. It scorched my tongue, burning as it made its way down my throat.

"Hot?" he asked, his eyes dancing in amusement.

"Yes." I lowered my cup and blew on it. "Very."

"So, we're supposed to form groups of five when we watch the comet." Chris pushed some hair off his forehead, and he continued, "I was thinking we could be in the same group. If you wanted to." His eyes filled with hope, and I had a feeling that he'd been waiting to ask all night.

"That sounds great." I smiled to show that I meant

it and wasn't just agreeing to be polite.

Kate headed over to us, and her eyes flashed with what looked like hurt when she looked at Chris. I blew on my hot chocolate again and took a step away from him. If Kate had feelings for him, I didn't want to give her the wrong idea. Because yes, Chris was nice, but I'd never thought of him as more than a friend.

"Do you all want to be in the same group?" She looked back and forth between Chris and me, toying with the ends of her hair.

"Yes," I said. "Of course."

Then someone else joined us—Blake. He stepped between Chris and me to grab his own hot chocolate, his gaze meeting mine with so much intensity that I could barely breathe. I took another sip of my drink, glad when it didn't burn my tongue, and waited for him to say something.

"Does your group have room for two more?" he asked.

"It's just the three of us," I said, my voice shaking. Hopefully he would think it was because of the cold and not because of his effect on me. "So yeah, we need two more."

The other person he was referring to must be Danielle. She stood at the edge of the deck with her arms crossed over her chest, a scowl plastered across her dark red lips. She reminded me of an angry lioness about to pounce on its prey. I broke my gaze away from hers, not wanting to look at her for a second longer. I couldn't help but think that she hated me, even though we'd never actually spoken to each other.

Given what Kate had told me about her, I should be scared. But I wasn't. Because according to Darius, I had powers, too. I was one of them. Danielle might mess around with humans, but she wouldn't hurt one of her own.

At least I hoped not.

Darius walked to the middle of the yard and cleared his throat. The chattering stopped.

"It's time to begin," he said, his voice carrying in every direction. "Please put down your drinks, find an empty place in the yard, and have your group gather in a circle. Take off your gloves if you're wearing them so they won't interfere with the energy passed between you and your group members."

Chris placed his half-empty cup down on the table. "Come on," he said, bounding off the deck and onto the yard.

Blake joined up with Danielle, and I followed them towards the spot that Chris had claimed. Kate trailed behind. Once we were all there, I looked up, gasping at what I saw.

The comet was already streaking through the sky, and it was more beautiful than I ever could have imagined. It shined yellow, with a hint of blue surrounding the edges, a trail of white growing wider behind it. It crawled at a steady pace. Unlike meteors, which flashed by in a second, the comet would stay visible for about an hour.

The comet was so beautiful that it was hard to believe it was real and not a special effect like in the movies.

The five of us joined hands, Blake on one side of me and Chris on the other. I'd expected to be more affected from Blake's touch than Chris's, but that wasn't the case. Both carried warmth, and a sense of security that I'd never felt before.

Darius didn't have to explain what to do next. I knew to close my eyes and focus on the energy surrounding us. It pulsated from every direction, and unlike the other day in homeroom, when I'd focused on gathering the energy and letting it in through my palms, it already existed inside me—in orbs of white that joined into a single whole. The light flowed out of my palms and through the rest of the circle. A rush of colors burst through me—green, blue, red, and yellow—twisting around each other like streamers in the wind.

The comet flashed through my mind, followed by a burst of power that exploded into a bright white light. Electricity shot through every inch of my body. Then the streams of colors unwound, each glowing with a brightness that it hadn't had at first. Each one fled out of my palms and returned to from wherever it came.

I pulled my hands out of Chris's and Blake's, my fists clenched so tightly that my nails dug into my skin. I relaxed my muscles and flexed my hands, opening my eyes and studying the others to see if they'd felt the same thing.

Their shocked looks said it all. Gone was the anger from Danielle's face, softened into what I could only describe as vulnerability. Chris stared up at the sky, his mouth open as he gazed at the comet. Kate seemed dazed, like she'd just woken up from a nap, and she looked around at all of us, her eyes wide. Blake seemed to have regained his composure, if he'd lost it at all, and he watched me closely, like he thought I could explain whatever had happened.

But I was as confused as they all looked. After all, I'd only known about this witchcraft stuff for a few days. I was the *least* qualified to provide any sort of explanation. Especially because on top of everything, their eyes all seemed brighter, as if enhanced. Danielle's were bluer, Kate's greener, Chris's more yellow, and Blake's a more intense shade of that burnt, reddish brown. My eyes had always been a pale, boring gray. But had they changed, too?

"What on Earth was that?" Chris finally broke the silence.

"You all felt it, too?" Kate's voice sounded weak, and she played with her hands, looking around the circle.

Danielle nodded. "If you're talking about that whole 'feeling like you were in a bathtub and someone dropped a hairdryer in it thing,' then yeah, I felt it." She flung her hair over her shoulder and crossed her arms over her chest, although she still didn't look as tough as she'd seemed before the comet.

"What was *supposed* to have happened?" I asked.

"None of us know." Kate gazed up at the sky, a distant look in her eyes. "We've never done a meditation under the Olympian Comet before."

"Obviously." I couldn't help but chuckle. "This comet comes around once every three thousand years. It's pretty safe to assume that you've never done this before, unless witches are immortal and no one's told me yet."

"We're not immortal." Blake laughed. "But I don't think any other group felt what we did. If they did, they're not acting like it."

I looked around the yard to see what he meant. The closest group to us consisted of freshmen. They were all frowning, their brows furrowed in disappointment. They must not have felt the energy jolt. Other students talked and laughed with each other. Some looked up at the comet as it made its way through the sky, their mouths open in awe. But not one person had a similar look of shock and confusion that I'd seen on the faces of the others in my group.

Suddenly, thunder cracked through the air, followed by a bright flash of lightning. Dark clouds covered the stars that had shined brightly only minutes before. They were so thick that the comet dimmed to a barely visible orb of light. The temperature felt like it had dropped at least ten degrees. Before I could process what was happening, sleet pounded down from the sky, the pinpricks of cold coming down so fast that they created a layer of ice on my skin and clothes.

I looked up in confusion, shielding my eyes from the sleet. I'd checked the weather before leaving. This hadn't been in the forecast.

"Everyone get inside!" Darius screamed, a boom of thunder drowning out his words.

My boots squished in the mud as I hurried across the yard, and I tried not to slip on the layer of ice forming on the ground. Finally, I made it inside the house. I removed my boots, adding them to the pile of dirty shoes next to the door, and placed my hands on my cheeks to warm them up.

Everyone packed into the living room as quickly as possible. Students had already squeezed onto the couches and armchairs surrounding the coffee table, so I plopped down on the rug with Chris and Kate. Blake and Danielle stood to the side, near the staircase. They were so involved in conversation that their heads nearly touched. Blake had his back to me, but I could see the irritation on Danielle's face. I wondered what they were fighting about—and if fighting was something they did often.

Once everyone was inside, Darius shut the porch doors and looked around the room. "I would have liked to stay outside and watch the comet for the entire hour, but obviously that isn't going to be possible," he said, clasping his hands in front of him. "So we're going to move on and discuss what occurred during the meditation. Did any of you notice a change in energy underneath the power of the comet?"

About half of the room nodded, and a senior guy with shaggy, light brown hair whose name I remembered was Patrick spoke up. "It felt like there was a lot more energy," he said with a shrug. "I can't explain it, but there was a difference. Like it was easier to access."

"Good." Darius nodded and looked around again. "Anyone else?"

"I finally felt some of the energy," a freshman girl

said from one of the couches. "It wasn't much, but it was definitely more than normal."

"That's wonderful." Darius smiled at her, and she sat up a bit straighter. "Hopefully you'll be able to take what you learned tonight and apply it to future lessons," he said. "Would anyone else like to volunteer what they experienced?"

I looked over at Kate. I'd assumed she would relish the opportunity to share our experience with the class, but she studied the rug, combing through the tassels. Danielle and Blake both leaned against the wall, not appearing like they were going to say anything, either.

Chris finally spoke up. "We got an electric jolt," he said, bringing his fingers together and pushing them apart to imitate a jolt of energy. "Everything was normal, then all these colors connected us together, and then BOOM—electric shock. It was pretty cool."

Darius furrowed his eyebrows. "What did the rest of you feel?" he asked, looking at Kate and me and then back to Blake and Danielle. "Was it like Chris said? A jolt of energy?"

"Yeah," Danielle said. "He pretty much covered it."

Darius looked back at me, and I nodded, as did Kate and Blake.

"Interesting," he mused, bringing his fingers to his chin and gazing out the window.

"Was that ... normal?" I finally asked.

"The Olympian Comet hasn't come around for three thousand years," he said. "There's no knowing what's 'normal.'"

I pulled my legs to my chest and wrapped my arms

around them. Wasn't Darius supposed to understand this stuff? The Elders were in charge, and if Darius—who was an Elder himself—didn't know what to expect, then we might never understand what had happened tonight in our circle.

I'd thought that coming here tonight would give me answers.

Instead, I was left with more questions than ever.

CHAPTER NINE

We talked for about an hour longer, then Darius ended the discussion and dismissed the class. Danielle didn't waste any time before marching over to Kate, Chris, and me, fire blazing in her eyes.

"Way to bring up what happened in front of everyone," she said to Chris, crossing her arms over her chest.

Chris stepped toward her, sticking his chin out. "What's the big deal?" he asked. "Darius asked us to talk about what we'd experienced, so I did. Aren't you curious about what happened, too?"

"Of course I'm curious." She rolled her eyes. "But we don't even know if we did anything or not. The last thing we want is everyone asking us questions."

Blake walked over to us before anyone could respond. "Hey, guys." He looked around at all of us, his eyes stopping on mine. "Are you all coming to the party tomorrow night?"

"What party?" I asked, surprised by the sudden change of subject.

He looked at Danielle and furrowed his eyebrows. "You didn't invite them yet?"

"She hadn't gotten to it." I doubted that Danielle had planned on inviting me anywhere, but a party was exactly the sort of break I needed from this witch stuff. It would be nice to do something normal for a change. "But I'd love to go."

"I'm in, too." Chris pushed his sleeves up to his elbows and flashed a boyish grin at Kate. "What about you, Kate?"

"Maybe." She shifted her feet and held her elbow with her hand. "I'll think about it."

"Great." Danielle didn't hide the sarcasm from her tone. "The party starts around eight. At my house."

"Sounds good." I stood straight and smiled, determined not to back down. "Thanks for the invite."

"We'll see you all tomorrow night." Blake turned to Danielle, who was standing as still as a statue, and rested his hand against her back. "You ready to go?"

"Yeah," she said, her eyes cold as ice. "We'll see you all tomorrow." She turned on her heel, threw her hair over her shoulder, and stomped after Blake as he walked out the front door.

"That girl has some serious issues," Kate said after they'd left.

"Understatement of the year." I laughed.

She laughed along with me, but then her eyes turned serious. "You don't actually plan on going tomorrow night, do you?"

"Why wouldn't I go?" I asked, even though I could think of a few reasons—the main one being that it was at Danielle's house and she clearly didn't want us there. But after whatever had happened between the five of us under the comet, I felt less afraid of Danielle than ever. "Blake invited us. The party will probably be fun, and it'll be easier for me to get to know people there than at school."

"I don't know ..." She pressed her lips together and held her elbow with her hand.

"Come on, Kate," Chris said. "Give the party a chance. You've lived here your whole life, and barely anyone knows you. It's about time you broke out of your shell."

"No one would force you to stay," I added. "If you get there and hate it, you can always leave. But isn't it better to go and see what happens than to stay home by yourself?"

"Fine," she gave in, shaking her head in defeat. "I'll go for a bit. But only because you guys insist."

CHAPTER TEN

Kate grudgingly allowed me to help her get ready for Danielle's party. Once we were finished, she looked amazing. The forest green top that was too tight on me fit her perfectly, the shimmery gold shadow I'd applied on her lids brought out the already enhanced green in her eyes, and her hair glowed after I'd taken my straightening iron to it and finished it off with some shine spray.

Once finished with her makeover, I gave my outfit a once-over in the mirror. The tight white dress accentuated the pale blondeness of my hair, which I'd styled in casual, beachy waves. I just hoped we wouldn't be outside for too long, or else my legs and arms would freeze.

Also, like the four others in the comet-watching group, my eye color had been enhanced, too. They were sharper, and more silver. It was striking, and I liked it, although I couldn't help feeling startled every time I caught sight of them in the mirror.

Kate had never been to Danielle's, so she took her time driving down the street, scanning the addresses on the mailboxes. It didn't take long to find it—mainly because of the cars packed in the driveway and along the street.

Our mouths dropped open when we saw Danielle's house. It looked like it belonged on the Athenian Acropolis instead of in a small town in Massachusetts. Two-story columns surrounded the double door entrance, and the triangular roof with engravings on the front made it look like the Parthenon infused with the White House. The door was unlocked, and Kate and I let ourselves in, stopping in our tracks as we looked around.

The huge foyer made me feel like I'd been transported into a Grecian temple. A staircase with a light blue rug running up it curved around the side, and a giant crystal chandelier hung from the ceiling. The top forty radio station played from speakers all over the house, loud enough to enjoy, but not so loud that it made it impossible to have conversations. There were clusters of people everywhere—some that I recognized from school—hanging out and chatting.

A handful of people said hi to Kate, but for the most part, no one noticed us. We wandered into the living room, hoping to find at least someone else from homeroom. A big group sat in the couches around a coffee table, and I smiled when I spotted Chris with them.

He waved Kate and me over and scooted to the end of the couch. I perched on the armrest, and Kate took the space next to him.

"For a minute I thought you guys weren't going to make it," Chris said, brushing his hair out of his eyes. "You know Stephanie and Patrick from homeroom." He pointed to two others that I recognized. I smiled and said hi, and then Chris turned to the couple on the sofa across from us. "And this is Anne and Matt. They're in Spanish with us."

I nodded, since what he really meant was, "they're not witches." Kate had explained to me earlier that while Danielle wasn't fond of humans, she invited them to her parties—at least the "popular" humans—so the party wouldn't look empty.

I answered the normal "new girl questions"—where I grew up, why I moved, what classes I was in, etc. Once finished with all that, I listened to their conversations, joining in whenever there was something to add. It felt so normal, and it was nice to get away from all of the witch talk.

But I still hadn't seen Blake. Figuring that he must be around somewhere, I wanted to walk around to try finding him. Casually, of course. I didn't want it to be obvious that I was looking forward to seeing him.

I hated that despite knowing he had a girlfriend, I hadn't been able to get him out of my mind. I didn't want to have these feelings for someone who was clearly off-limits. But Blake had invited me to the party, so saying hi and letting him know that I was here wasn't wrong. It was simply being polite.

At least the excuse made me feel not *as* terrible about these feelings for him that I couldn't control.

"I'm going to get a drink," I said when the conversation lulled. "Do you all want anything?"

Chris and the others already had drinks, and Kate shook her head no.

I headed for the kitchen, weaving in and out of clumps of people talking. Danielle's kitchen was huge—it would have been bright and airy if it weren't packed with people. Everyone seemed to be helping themselves to drinks, so I walked over to the fridge and browsed my options. The only sodas left were those old-styled glass bottles with the aluminum tops that are impossible to open, so I grabbed one in the hope that there would be an opener nearby.

"I was wondering if you would show." The smooth voice behind me was unmistakably Blake's. Just hearing him speak made my heart race, and I turned to face him, trying to keep my face relaxed so he wasn't aware of how flustered I became in his presence.

He held his gaze with mine, his eyes full of so much intensity that I almost forgot to breathe. Before I realized what he was doing, he grabbed my drink, popped it open using the side of the counter, and handed it back to me.

"Thanks." My hand shook when I took it back from him, and I took a sip to calm my nerves. "Of course I showed. The last few days have been crazy, so it's nice to be able to do something normal for a change."

He leaned against the counter, resting his elbows on top of it. Some people started cheering about something at the other side of the kitchen, but he kept his focus solely on me. "It's been crazier than usual with the comet yesterday," he said, his arm only inches away from mine. My pulse quickened, and I had to remind myself to breathe. "Plus it's not every day that someone new transfers into our homeroom. Especially someone with no training, who has no idea about our history. I think some people are jealous about how quickly you're picking up on everything."

"Without Kate, I would be completely lost," I told him. "She's helping me study, so I can get on track for the honors classes. I'm picking up on everything much faster than I thought I would. Kate claims it's because the yellow energy is helping me focus."

"What we can do is definitely useful," he said.

"Yeah." I shivered, thinking about the story Kate had told me—about how Danielle had used her powers to injure that girl. I didn't know if Blake did things like that as well, but I wanted to make it clear that I planned on using my powers for good. "And who knows," I added. "Maybe I'll be able to use my new abilities to improve my tennis game."

"Of course you're a tennis player." He smiled, and I wondered why he seemed so amused. "How long have you been playing?"

"About ten years," I said it casually, even though I knew it was a long time. "I was on the team back

71

home. I've been out for a few weeks because of a knee injury, but my knee got better when I moved here, and I'm more than ready to start again. I figured I would try out for the Kinsley team this spring."

"You'll get in," he said confidently. "Danielle's only been playing for five years and she's number one on varsity. Of course, like everyone in our homeroom she has certain ... advantages. But I'm guessing you would get on the team even without those."

"Maybe." I smiled at the thought of playing again. However, while getting on the team should be doable given my experience, snagging the number one spot from Danielle might be tough. Blake had basically confirmed that she used her powers to help her game. And despite my natural tennis ability, I wasn't at her level when it came to using our powers—yet.

Blake glanced at something behind me, and a shadow passed over his eyes.

I turned around and saw Danielle heading towards us. She looked like Aphrodite risen from the ocean in her sparkly sapphire dress that clung to her every curve. Her eyes matched her dress, looking even brighter than they had on the night of the comet. In her heels, she towered over me, and I couldn't help shrinking under her gaze.

"What are you two talking about?" Her icy tone sent chills up my spine. She scooted closer to Blake and rested her hand on his arm, her face hardening in an unspoken message that he was hers and she didn't want me anywhere near him.

"Nicole was telling me that she played tennis at her

old school," he said. "She wants to try out for the team here."

"Really?" She raised an eyebrow. "Did Blake also mention that I'm on first spot varsity?"

"Yeah." I nodded, not bringing up that I'd been first spot varsity on my old team before getting injured, too. I had a feeling she wouldn't take the news well.

"I was about to tell her about the indoor winter team at the tennis club," Blake continued, turning to me. "Most of the girls on the school team join it to prepare for tennis season in the spring."

Danielle huffed, and despite her obvious annoyance that Blake was giving me so much information, I bounced at the prospect of playing tennis again.

"When does that start?" I asked.

"Tuesday," Danielle said coldly. "You could come and ask the coach about trying out, but don't expect much. She's strict, and try-outs were in December. She's already assigned spots."

"It can't hurt to try," I said. "Even if there's not a place for me on the team right now, I could put a weekly game together at the tennis club, just for fun."

"Perhaps." Danielle studied her nails. I had a feeling that if I were looking for volunteers to play with, she wouldn't be raising her hand anytime soon.

Blake stood perfectly still next to her, his eyes hard. I wanted to continue talking with him, but since Danielle wasn't budging from her perch, I excused myself and headed back to the living room.

Kate and Chris were still there, now surrounded by a larger group of people. I sat back on the arm of the couch and re-joined the conversation, talking and laughing with them as if we'd known each other for longer than a few days.

For the first time since moving to Kinsley, I felt somewhat normal—like I was finally finding my place here.

And I couldn't shake the feeling that it wasn't going to last.

CHAPTER ELEVEN

The moment I stepped inside the tennis club and heard the familiar popping of balls against rackets, I felt at home. I twirled my racket in my hand, and not wanting to waste any time, I walked over to the information desk. A tall, blond man was folding shirts on the counter. While older, he was in good shape, and I assumed he taught some classes at the club.

"Is the coach for the girls team here yet?" I asked, wishing I'd found out the coach's name ahead of time.

"Martha!" he called toward an open door in the back. "You've got someone here for you."

A stout lady with shoulder-length gray hair walked through the door. "Yes?" she asked, pursing her lips like she just ate a sour candy.

My hands shook, and I tightened my grip around my racket. I'd assumed that Danielle was trying to scare me away when she warned me that the coach was tough, but now I was starting to think that she meant it.

"Hi." I plastered a smile on my face and tried to appear confident, even though my insides were squirming. "I'm Nicole Cassidy—I just moved here, and heard that you're in charge of the junior team. I'm a sophomore at Kinsley High, and since I hadn't moved to town yet during regular try-outs, I was wondering if there was any way for me to try out now?"

She held her pen to her chin and eyed up my racket. It was high quality—a birthday present from my dad. "How long have you been playing?" she finally asked.

"Ten years," I told her, standing straighter. "I played varsity for my school in Georgia. This year *and* last year."

She placed her pen down and studied me. "You played varsity as a freshman?"

"Yes." My cheeks heated—hopefully she didn't think I was making it up. I'd always excelled in tennis, but I didn't like to brag about it. If she watched me play she would see for herself.

"You can try out for the team today," she decided, picking up the clipboard and hugging it to her side. "I can't promise you a spot, since our team is very competitive, but I'll see how you do and we'll go from there."

Despite trying to remain calm, a grin spread across

my face. "Thank you!" I exclaimed, resisting the urge to give her a big hug. She didn't seem like the touchy-feely type.

She wrote something on her clipboard. "Be on the court at 4:00 PM sharp," she instructed.

"Will do."

She nodded, and feeling like she was done with the conversation, I walked to the balcony overlooking the courts. On the closest one, a group of younger kids aimed balls towards cones on the opposite end. I smiled while watching them, since that had been my favorite drill when I was that age. I'd picked it up immediately—accuracy had always been my strength. All you had to do was look where you wanted the ball to go, aim, and hit. Easy.

"So, you decided to show up after all," Danielle said from behind me.

"Yeah." I turned and held her gaze, balancing my racket in front of me. With her hair slicked back into a ponytail, her eyes looked more catlike than normal. "I talked with the coach, and she's letting me try out."

Danielle's expression hardened. "How nice of her," she said, her tone sugary sweet. "Good luck." She turned on her heel and strutted towards a group of girls who had just arrived, swishing her skirt for extra emphasis.

A few minutes later, everyone gathered on the court. Coach Peterson informed the team that I would be trying out, and that she would be observing me as if it were a normal practice. Before anyone could comment, she told us to run five laps to warm up.

Following everyone else's lead, I dropped my racket and started to run. It felt great to run again—hearing the slaps of my sneakers hitting the pavement, feeling the air whiz through my hair as it flew behind my head, and the adrenaline rush of my heart pumping faster as I gained speed. My previously injured knee didn't so much as twinge. It felt amazing—like I was flying.

I was first to finish, lapping a few of the other girls on the way. Danielle finished second. She picked her racket back up and did some stretches, refusing to look at me.

After everyone completed their laps, Coach Peterson divided us into groups of four to warm up. I breathed a sigh of relief when she didn't put me in the same group as Danielle.

The girls in my group were decent players, but discovering their weaknesses was easy. It wouldn't be difficult to strategize how to beat them in a game. Since we were just warming up, I didn't hit as hard as I would have normally, but they didn't come close to challenging me. My guess was that they had low spots on JV.

After twenty minutes, Coach Peterson blew her whistle. "Time's up!" she shouted, her voice carrying through all six courts. "Take a water break, and then we'll play some games."

I dropped my racket in the hall and ran to the water fountain, but Coach Peterson called my name before I could get in line. I jogged over to her, my heart pounding with each step. I had to relax. I'd just shown some solid hitting. She had no reason not to want me on the team.

"Very impressive warm-up," she said with a hint of a smile. "I'd like to see how you do with the girls who play varsity singles. From there, I'll figure out where to place you on the team."

"Great." I grinned at how she said *where* she would place me on the team, not *if*. I had a spot. I would definitely be able to play. "Thank you so much."

"You'll be a strong addition." She looked down at her watch, her face hardening again. "Go get some water, and I'll let the other girls know about the changes."

I nodded and hurried back over to the fountain. One of the girls I'd warmed up with gave me a high five, and most of the other girls introduced themselves, welcoming me to the team.

"Congratulations," Danielle said to me as she approached, as icy as ever. "Coach told me that you're going to be playing with me and some of the other girls on varsity. This should be ... interesting, to say the least."

"Thanks." I smiled, too happy to deal with her negativity. Luckily, it was my turn at the water fountain, so I lowered my head to take a sip, pushing the button next to the faucet.

The water spurted out at full speed, splashing everywhere and getting all over my face and hair. I shrieked and backed away, wiping the water off my cheeks and blinking it out of my eyes.

Danielle snickered, and I glared at her, squeezing

the water from my hair onto the floor. She looked so smug, as if she had done it.

But that was impossible. Because like Darius had said on my first day, our powers were mental, not physical. Danielle couldn't be responsible for what had just happened. It must have been a glitch in the piping system.

The water came out at a normal speed when I tried again, and after a few sips I grabbed my racket and headed back to where everyone was gathered around the coach. Danielle laughed again, but I held my head higher, not looking back at her. Getting a spot on the team was a *good* moment. I wouldn't let her ruin it.

"You're going to be on court one," Coach told me. "Grab your racket and get started. I'll decide where to place you after observing you play."

The other three girls were already there when I arrived. Danielle had teamed up with a senior from homeroom named Kara. They smirked at each other when they saw me, as if confident they were going to beat me. I took a deep breath and ran my fingers over the strings of my racket. I had to stay focused on my game. Danielle might have an advantage with her powers, but I had five years of playing on her. I should be able to handle this.

The tall, blonde girl on the other side of the court, who I figured would be my partner, smiled and waved me over. "I'm Jessica," she introduced herself.

"Hi." I smiled back at her. "I'm Nicole."

"I know," she said. "We have homeroom together."

Right after she said it, I recognized her—she was

the quiet girl in back who'd answered one of Darius's questions on my first day.

I suspected it wasn't a coincidence that the three highest ranked girls on the team were all in my homeroom.

"You can serve first," Danielle said to me, tossing a few balls in my direction.

"Sure." I caught them and walked to the baseline. What did Danielle have up her sleeve by letting me start? The serving team always had the advantage.

I highly doubted that she'd offered out of the kindness of her heart, but all I could do was relax and play my best. So I tossed the ball in the air, throwing my whole body into the serve as I aimed and swung.

The ball popped against the rim of my racket and fell into the net.

"Fault." Danielle squared her shoulders and smirked. "Good try, though."

I didn't reply to her fake compliment, instead bouncing the next ball on the ground in preparation to serve again. That had just been a warm-up. This time I would hit a serve so strong that Danielle wouldn't have time to blink as it shot past her.

I tossed the ball up again, but my racket connected with it too late. It arced through the air and landed behind the base line.

"Double fault." Danielle flicked her hair over her shoulder and smiled triumphantly. "Love-15."

I glared at her for calling the score. That was supposed to be the responsibility of the server. Meaning: me.

I twirled my racket in an attempt to quench my nerves. There had to be something I could do to relax. Then I remembered the colors that Darius had written on the board. Kate had made me memorize each one during our first study session. Maybe one of them could help?

I decided on blue, the most calming of the colors. If I could harness blue energy, maybe I could loosen up and play at my potential.

It might not work. But it couldn't hurt to try.

I shifted from one foot to the other and closed my eyes, hoping it looked like I was just trying to center myself. But really, I pictured blue in my mind. I pulled it toward me until the color surrounded me, and I imagined it entering through my palms, filling my body and soothing my nerves.

With my hand gripped around my racket, I could tell that something about it felt fuzzy and off—perhaps because I hadn't used it in so long. So I sent some of the blue energy into my racket as well.

Then I tossed the ball up again and hit it.

It arced through the air and landed exactly where I'd aimed. The shot was decent, but the lack of force behind it allowed Kara to smash it to the middle of the court where neither Jessica nor I could reach it.

It was far from perfect. But at least it was better.

The game continued in the same way, with me either missing my target or hitting an accurate but slow serve that was easy for Danielle or Kara to return with force. Coach Peterson watched from the sidelines, frowning. I couldn't blame her. I was disappointed with my playing, too.

Since imagining blue energy had helped slightly, I reminded myself about what *all* of the colors represented. Red didn't only increase attraction and desire—it increased confidence as well. So I called the red energy into my body, feeling refreshed a second later. Then I thought about yellow and how it increases focus. A surge of yellow entered my palms, sharpening my attentiveness on the game. Lastly, I thought about blue again, trying to calm down and not let the frustration at my poor playing mess me up even more.

The three colors flowed through my body, and I tightened my grip on my racket, sending the colors through it as well. Energy hummed through me, crackling with power. I bounced the ball a few times on the court, and my senses felt sharper. Faster.

I was ready.

Suddenly I was playing better than ever. I was in control of every shot—each one full of strength and precision. It didn't take long for Jessica and me to take the lead.

Eventually, Coach blew her whistle to signify the end of practice. She was waiting for me at the exit of the courts, and I walked over to her, my heart pounding with anticipation.

"I'm going to chalk that first game up to nerves," she said before I had a chance to speak. "I haven't decided on your starting position yet, but I'll watch you on Thursday and see how it goes. If you play the same way you did for the majority of the day, it's safe to say that you can expect a top spot."

"Thank you," I said, able to breathe for the first time since walking over. "I can't wait to be a part of the team."

"Don't thank me." She finally smiled. "You earned it."

For the most part, I agreed with her. But I'd *really* messed up during that first game. And I couldn't stop thinking about what Kate had told me about Danielle—that she used her abilities to negatively affect others. Specifically, on girls who talked to Blake.

Had Danielle used her powers to mess me up?

And if she had, was there anything I could do to protect myself from her?

CHAPTER TWELVE

"You should watch where you put your racket during tennis practice," Blake said to me the next day in ceramics. We were working on our coil pots from yesterday, and we had a table to ourselves. I wondered if Blake was putting out some sort of energy that encouraged everyone to sit as far away from him as possible.

Well—everyone but me, of course.

"What do you mean?" I asked.

"Just that some people—specifically certain ones in our homeroom—might take advantage of the fact that you left your racket alone on the court."

I jerked back, my eyes widening at what he'd implied. "You mean that Danielle messed with my racket?"

"I'm not saying any names," he said. "I'm just telling you to be more careful."

I wanted to know more, but it was a touchy subject, given that she was his girlfriend. "Thanks," I said instead. "Next time, I won't let my racket out of my sight."

"You do that," he said. "But ... don't you want to learn how to get back at her?"

I held his gaze, wondering if he meant it. He should be on Danielle's side—not mine. Was this some sort of trick? I didn't think so, but even if it wasn't, the last thing I needed was to start a fight with Danielle. I might be getting the hang of harnessing energy, but Danielle was more powerful than me. I needed to be careful.

"I don't want to 'get back' at her," I said carefully. "But if there's a way to defend myself against whatever she's doing, I would like to learn how to do that."

He leaned forward so his face was only inches away from mine, and goosebumps traveled over my arms. "There is," he said, lowering his voice. "All you have to do is use white energy. It's the strongest color out there, but it's the hardest to harness. If you can do it, and if you direct it properly, it can take spells off of objects. The tricky part is knowing what objects have been tampered with. And it's difficult to remove the energy if someone more powerful than you put it there. But you've got natural talent. Even Darius is impressed."

I ripped off a piece of clay from the chunk on the

table and rolled another coil. "White energy," I repeated. "What about concentrating on a few colors at once? I did that with three of them and it helped."

"Since combining all of the colors makes white energy, I guess three might do something," he said. "And if it worked, that means you've got as much power as Danielle—maybe even more."

"So you admit it was Danielle!" I smiled in triumph.

His jaw tensed, and he looked down at the table, refusing to meet my eyes.

"I won't tell anyone," I said. "I promise."

He studied me, like he was trying to figure out if I was trustworthy or not. "Good," he finally said. "Because if Danielle found out that I was trying to help you, she might take it out on you. And while I doubt she would do anything too terrible—after all, you're one of us— I don't want you getting hurt."

My cheeks heated, and I feared they were turning bright pink. Why would Blake go behind his girlfriend's back to help me? I wanted to think that he was just as attracted to me as I was to him, but I didn't want to get my hopes up. Because he and Danielle were still together. So Blake and I couldn't be anything more than friends.

I looked down at the table and focused on rolling another coil. My emotions were probably splattered so much on my face that they would betray me completely.

"So, have you thought any more about the night of the comet?" I asked to fill the silence.

"Constantly," he said, his hands moving faster as he

worked. "I don't know why—or how—but my abilities have changed since that night."

"What do you mean?" I asked.

"I can't show you here." He glanced around the room, as if afraid of someone listening. "At least not without freaking everyone out and getting in trouble with the Elders."

"Okay," I said. "But can you at least *tell* me?"

"No," he said. "This is something that needs to be seen. Come with me after class and I'll show you."

His eyes darkened, and my breath caught with the realization that whatever he was planning on showing me was serious—and that for whatever reason, he was choosing to come to me with it. He trusted me.

And even though I knew I shouldn't, I trusted him, too.

CHAPTER THIRTEEN

The rest of ceramics class dragged on forever.

"Are you ready for what I'm about to show you?" Blake asked after the bell finally rang.

"After all of this build up, it better be good," I joked, although I was only halfway kidding.

We gathered our stuff and headed out of the classroom. "Come on," he said, walking the opposite way down the hall—toward the back of the building. It led to a dead end, but I followed anyway, trusting that he knew where he was going. He stopped at the door to the back stairwell, opening it and tilting his head for me to go first.

My arm brushed his as I walked through, a rush of heat flowing from his skin and into mine. My breath caught in my chest, and I pulled away, moving aside to give him space to enter. The stairwell was dim and unfinished, and he inched the door shut, closing out the rest of the world.

The chattering of the last kids walking down the hall quieted, and it was just the two of us. Alone. My heart was pounding so hard that he could probably hear it, and even though I'd wanted to be alone with Blake since the moment I first saw him, I needed to control whatever I was feeling for him. Nothing could happen between us. At least not right now, while he had a girlfriend.

"So ... what did you want to show me?" I asked, pulling my sleeves over my hands and wrapping my arms around myself.

"This." He removed something from his pocket and held it in front of him. It was a clay pendant of a miniature sun, about the size of his palm. The dark gray color of the clay made it obvious that it hadn't gone in the kiln yet.

"It's beautiful." I let my fingers hover over it, afraid to touch it. "You made it?"

"Yes." He nodded. "I did."

"But why take it now, before firing it in the kiln?" I asked. "If you don't fire it, it'll eventually crumble."

"I'm going to show you something," he said softly, his gaze so focused on mine that I had to lean against the wall to steady myself. "Promise me you won't freak out."

"I promise." I somehow kept my voice from shaking. "Given everything that I've learned recently, it would take a lot to freak me out now."

"Fair point." He reached into his pocket and pulled out a black lighter. "You ready?"

"Yes." I swallowed and held his gaze. "I'm ready."

He flicked on the lighter, and it sparked to life, casting a glow across his face that made him look like he was from another world. Then he lowered the flame to the pendant—which was still sitting in his hand.

"What are you doing?" I gasped and reached forward to stop him. "You'll burn yourself."

"No." He pulled away from me, and as the flames touched his skin, he didn't even flinch. "Watch."

The fire grew taller and brighter, and then he turned the lighter off. The flames should have gone out. Instead, they turned blue, growing hotter and burning stronger than ever, fully surrounding the pendant. He was holding fire, and his hand wasn't burning. He was *controlling* the flames. Which, according to what I'd learned this week about how our abilities worked, wasn't supposed to be possible.

But I couldn't deny what I was seeing in front of my eyes.

Finally the fire died out, and he held the pendant up for me to see. The clay sun had hardened completely. If I didn't know better, I would have thought that it had been in the kiln for hours.

"How did you do that?" I brushed my finger over the pendant, but it was scorching hot, and I yanked my hand away.

"I don't know." He stared at the tiny sun, looking as transfixed as I felt. "Yesterday I was lighting the fireplace in my house and it felt like I could make the flames move like I wanted. I wasn't sure if I was imagining it or not, so I went to my room to experiment." His jaw hardened, and he raised his gaze to meet mine. "I wasn't imagining it. I could control the fire."

"But that's impossible," I said. "We can't affect the physical world like that. Right?"

"The only explanation I could come up with is that something happened when we felt that jolt under the comet, and whatever it was changed us," he said. "It gave me this ability."

"Maybe," I said. "Or maybe this was something you would have been able to do even without the comet."

"I've never heard of anything like this," he said. "Then I remembered a bit about Hephaestus—the Greek god of fire—and I looked him up. Not even *he* could control fire with his mind." He glanced at the pendant again, and then re-focused on me, his eyes burning with intensity. "I thought that since this all started when you moved here, you might know what's going on."

"Last week, I didn't know that witches existed," I reminded him. "All of this is new to me. I'm the *least* qualified person for you to ask."

"But you were with us under the comet, and I know you're picking up on how to use your abilities abnormally fast," he said. "That's why I had to talk to you today. Have you been able to do anything like I just did with the fire? Anything that affects the physical world?"

Disappointment surged through my chest as I realized why he'd brought me here. Until now, despite the complications, I'd hoped he was interested in me and wanted to spend time with me. That he thought I was someone he could trust. That he was as drawn to me as much as I was to him.

But he didn't feel that way at all. He was just trying to get information from me.

I shouldn't have expected anything more. And as I was standing here, crushed, he was waiting for me to explain his newfound ability. I had to set him straight. I was no one special. And I certainly didn't have the answers he thought I did.

"I haven't been able to do anything like that." I focused on the pendant, purposefully avoiding looking at him. "Even if something *were* different with my abilities, I wouldn't know, since I didn't even know I had abilities until a week ago."

"What about Kate or Chris?" he asked. "Have they mentioned anything unusual?"

"No." I shook my head. "But something strange did happen at tennis yesterday..." I paused, hoping I wasn't about to say something totally off base. But he nodded for me to continue, so I did. "I was getting a drink of water, and the fountain went all crazy on me, like it was possessed. Danielle was standing right behind me. She was upset that I might get her spot on the team."

His eyebrows knit together. "Do you think she got jealous and doused you with water? That she *controlled* it? Like I controlled the fire?"

"I don't know." I ran my hands through my hair, since it sounded silly when he put it that way. "Maybe. Or maybe the water fountain was faulty, and the timing was a coincidence."

We both looked at each other, saying nothing. I could tell that neither of us believed it.

"Thanks for telling me," he finally said. "I'll ask Danielle about it later."

I nodded and glanced around the empty stairwell. "We should head to class," I said, shifting my feet. "We're late."

I didn't actually want to leave—I would have skipped class entirely to spend time with Blake—but being alone with him was just going to get my hopes up. I had to be stronger than that. I had to fight whatever I was feeling for him. Because he didn't return those feelings, and it would be easier for me once I accepted that.

I reached for the door, determined with my resolve, but he held his hand out to stop me.

"Hold on," he said, and I was helpless to do anything but still at his touch. "I didn't make this for myself. I made it for you." He lifted the sun pendant, motioning for me to take it.

I grazed my fingers along its surface, studying the details he'd engraved. A small face sat in the center, and two layers of rays extended in all directions. It was beautiful.

"Wow," I said softly, taking it from him. It was still warm from the fire, and it pulsed at my touch. "Thank you."

"I made it for you because you remind me of the sun."

I took a sharp breath inward. If he were anyone else, I would have thought this meant something. That *I* meant something to him. But he had a girlfriend, and I didn't want to be a side-girl, or a fleeting fascination.

I wanted the real thing.

So I stepped back and slipped the pendant into my bag. "We should go," I said.

Disappointment flashed over his eyes, but he opened the door, motioning for me to go first.

Everyone stared at us when we entered class late. Luckily, Darius believed us when we said we had extra clean up duty at the end of ceramics. We took our normal seats and settled in, but it was impossible for me to focus. My thoughts kept wandering to Blake and the small clay pendant in my bag.

I reminded him of the sun.

For some reason, the comparison just felt ... right.

CHAPTER FOURTEEN

In homeroom on Friday morning, every desk had a glass of water on top of it. I sat next to Kate, eyeing my glass curiously. I suspected that I wasn't supposed to drink it.

"Something strange happened with my lab experiment for bio," she said the moment I sat down. "You know how out of the three plants we're growing, the one with no direct sunlight is supposed to grow the slowest? And the one with the most sunlight should grow the fastest?"

"Yeah..." I said, wondering where she was going with this. It didn't take a genius to figure out how the results for the lab would turn out.

"I got to school early to check on my plants." Her

eyes went distant, like she was seeing what had happened again in her mind. "They were larger than anyone else's, but get this—the one with no light grew just as much as the one *with* light." She wrung her hands together, chewing on her lower lip. "That's not how the lab was supposed to turn out. It doesn't make sense."

I searched my mind for an explanation, but couldn't think of anything. "Maybe someone moved your plants around?" I finally said.

"No." She shook her head. "We labeled them ahead of time. They weren't mixed up."

The bell rang before I could come up with another possible answer, and Darius walked to the front of the room. He clasped his hands behind him and looked around.

"Today we'll be working on directing energy into a drink, such as water, to affect someone's mood when they ingest it," he told us. "I want you to focus on an approved color of your choosing. If you're an upperclassman you should have this down by now, so this should be practice. I'd like to see the sophomores getting the hang of it, and freshmen, don't feel badly if you find it difficult." He scanned his eyes over the freshman in the front row. "If you still haven't succeeded in gathering energy, please work on that instead. Skills build on each other, and you'll need that one to be successful with this."

He sat down at his desk, which I took as a cue to begin.

I decided to use the color orange. A main quality

orange represented was strength, and with everything going on in my life, it couldn't hurt to have more of that.

Ready to start, I looked around to see what everyone else was doing. Some students had closed their eyes, and others stared at their glasses with such intensity that it looked like they were trying to make them combust with a single thought.

I closed my eyes and immediately sensed the orange energy around me. The tingling started in my palms—rushing inwards like waves of light traveling through my body. The orbs of energy grew larger, swirling together until they felt like they were going to burst through my skin. Unable to contain the energy for any longer, I opened my eyes and touched the glass, shooting orange beams of imaginary light out of my palms.

A loud crack echoed through the room as the glass exploded, shards and water flying in every direction.

I stared at the place where the glass had been, my eyes wide, my palms flat on the table. Shards of glass were everywhere, and there was a puddle of water in the center of my desk, inching closer to the edge.

Had I really been responsible for *that*? Everyone stared at me, and heat rushed to my face, but this time it wasn't because of the energy. I just wanted my classmates to stop gaping at me like I was some sort of freak-witch.

"I knocked over the glass," I lied. "It was an accident. I'm fine."

Kate appeared in front of me with a roll of paper

towels, and she did her best to gather the glass and mop up the water. I tore off some towels to help.

"Nicole." Kate's voice wavered, and she pointed at my wrist. "You're bleeding."

I looked at where she was pointing and froze. A piece of glass had embedded itself inside of my forearm, blood seeping out from the sides. The shard was about the size of my baby toe—big enough to cause damage, but small enough that you had to be close to notice it. It stung, but it didn't hurt. Not as badly as I would have expected. It was like I was looking at someone else's injury—not my own.

Maybe I was in shock.

Not wanting to bring more attention to myself than I already had, I lowered my arm under the desk so no one could see. Homeroom was almost over. After the bell rang I could walk quietly to the nurse's office and get cleaned up. There was no need to cause more of a commotion.

Then the pain hit, like a swarm of bees gathering around the cut and stinging at the same time. Not knowing what else to do, I closed my eyes and yanked the glass out of my arm, biting my lower lip to stop myself from screaming. Once it was out, I dropped it on the floor and held my hand over the wound to slow the bleeding. It burned so badly, like someone had set my arm on fire.

My head spun, and I pressed harder on the cut, trying to hold the skin together. What good was being a witch if I couldn't fix this?

Maybe I *could* fix it. I didn't know the limits of what

I could do. And so, remembering what Blake had told me about white energy and how it could fix things, I gathered as many colors as I could, pictured them combining to form white, and directed them towards the cut. I let the light flow out of my palm and into my arm, imagining my skin stitching and melding back together.

Soon the throbbing calmed, and I lifted my hand, forcing myself to look.

My skin was now perfectly smooth.

I had no time to think about what I'd done. Instead, I grabbed a wet paper towel and rubbed it over my arm, cleaning off the blood. There wasn't too much, but it was enough that people would ask questions when they couldn't find an obvious wound. After cleaning up, I put the bloodied towel in my bag, which was gross, but I needed to hide the evidence. I was about to slide on my hoodie when Kate grabbed my arm.

"Let me see that." She rotated it to search for the cut. When she saw that it wasn't there, she stared at me, her eyes wide in question.

"See what?" I tilted my head, trying to play it off like everything was fine. Others had gathered around to help clean up, and I didn't want them to know what had happened. They didn't need *another* reason to think I was a freak. Hopefully Kate understood that I would tell her later, and wouldn't say anything now.

She dropped my arm and frowned. "Nothing," she mumbled, gathering the wet towels and taking them to the trash.

Once she was gone, Chris scooted his chair closer to mine. "How did you do that?" he asked, nearly bouncing out of his seat.

"Do what?" My brain felt like it was in a haze. I looked at the clock to see how long it had been. Only a minute had passed.

How could all of that have happened in such a short amount of time?

"Your glass looked like it spontaneously combusted." He laughed and pushed some hair off his forehead.

I relaxed, realizing he was talking about the glass exploding and not the cut on my arm. "It didn't spontaneously combust," I said, trying to laugh it off. "I knocked it over, and it broke."

"You must have knocked it over pretty hard." He looked at the place where the shards had been and shook his head.

I shrugged, since that wasn't what had happened, and Chris seemed to know it, too.

Darius stepped to the front of the room and cleared his throat. "I'm going to let you all leave early today," he said, and everyone cheered. Then he turned to me, his eyes sharp. "Nicole, please meet with me here after school. I'd like to go over some of the material you need to catch up on."

I nodded, since I didn't have much of a choice. I also didn't know how much Darius had seen.

All I knew was that what had just happened to me definitely wasn't normal.

And that he was the only one who might have

answers.

CHAPTER FIFTEEN

The rest of the day passed in a haze. It was like there was cotton in my brain and I was watching everything happen around me instead of being there myself. I was more than ready for the weekend, so when the final bell rang, all I wanted was to go home. But I couldn't skip the meeting with Darius.

The door to the library classroom was open when I arrived. Darius sat at his desk, reading something from a piece of paper. He looked up when he heard me enter.

"Nicole," he said, removing his glasses and placing them down. "Thank you for meeting with me. I had hoped to talk with you one-on-one before now, but things have been rather hectic since you arrived."

I felt bad that I hadn't come to him sooner. It just seemed weird to talk to a teacher when I had friends like Kate, Chris, and Blake to help me along. Of course Darius wasn't a *normal* teacher, but maybe I'd avoided talking with him because it would mean admitting that all of this was real.

But at this point, did I really have a choice?

"Sorry," I apologized, shoving my hands into the back pockets of my jeans. "Things have been really crazy with moving and all."

"It must be difficult to adjust to so many changes," he said, gesturing to the chair next to his desk. "Please sit. I'd like to show you something."

I made my way across the room and sat in the chair, crossing my legs and waiting for him to continue. But instead of saying anything, he pushed the paper he was reading towards me. I leaned forward to get a better look.

It wasn't actually paper. It was more like parchment—ancient and yellowed—and it only had a paragraph of writing on it in thick black ink. I ran my finger along the bottom of it, surprised by how rough it felt under my skin, and skimmed the perfect calligraphy:

In the beginning of the new year, the Olympian comet will cross the sky and the wall will grow thin. Five representing each part of the world will work together to restore the balance, the power of the Aether igniting them. The Journey will lead them East on the path to the Shadows, which will serve as their guide.

It made no sense, and re-reading it didn't help. Only

the comet had any relevance. The rest might as well have been written in Ancient Greek.

I looked back up at Darius and shrugged. "I don't understand what this means."

He picked it up, locked it into a drawer, and pulled out a piece of paper that looked like it was from this century. It had the same thing written on it. "A girl named Abigail Goode wrote this a little more than three hundred years ago," he said. "She was a witch who lived in Kinsley, and this is believed to be a prophecy. The Elder in charge of the Kinsley area— which would be myself—keeps watch over the original. This is a copy." He placed the newer looking version in front of me. "I want you to hold onto it for now."

"What?" I did a double take and sat back. "Why me?"

He studied me and folded his hands over his desk. "You've exemplified extreme natural ability with your power," he said simply. "In just over a week you've mastered what takes most students months to learn. And what you did in class today..." His eyes lingered on the spot on my arm where the cut had been, and I covered it with my other hand. "Like I told you on your first day, our powers are mental, not physical. But you made that glass explode. Which shouldn't be possible, but you did it."

I opened my mouth to protest—to give him the same excuse I'd given to Chris—but he held a hand up to stop me.

"I saw what happened, and it won't do either of us any good for you to deny it," he said kindly. "I hope you know that I want to help you. I've talked with a few of the Head Elders, and while they have their theories, I believe you're the key to deciphering this prophecy."

"Hold on." My eyes widened at the possibility. "You think *I* can figure that out?"

He nodded, his expression serious. "Yes, I think you can figure it out," he said. "Because I believe you're the one spoken of in the prophecy."

I pointed to the paper. "There's no person mentioned here."

"I'll let you figure that out for yourself," he said. "But I have to leave and take care of some business at home. Good luck, Nicole." He gathered his briefcase and left the room, leaving me alone with the paper.

"Thanks," I muttered, shaking my head and picking up the supposed prophecy.

Only a week and a half into a new school, and not only was I a freaky super-witch who made a glass explode in class, but I also had extra homework.

CHAPTER SIXTEEN

Re-reading the prophecy didn't help me understand it, and I left the room after about five minutes of failed attempts. The library was nearly empty except for a few scattered students. I headed for the doors, but the sight of one person in particular made me stop in place.

Blake sat at a nearby table, absorbed in his history textbook. He leaned back in the chair, one knee propped against the edge of the table to balance the book on his leg. In the week and a half that I'd known him, I'd never seen him look so focused. Maybe he'd put yellow energy into his water that morning and had chugged it to help him study.

Which might have made sense, except that we

shared the same history class, and we didn't *have* any tests or papers due in the near future. So he had no reason to be here.

Unless he was waiting to talk to me.

Feeling braver than usual—perhaps because of the orange energy I'd gathered this morning—I slid into the seat next to him. "You didn't strike me as a 'stay after school on a Friday to do homework' type of guy," I said, leaning back and making myself comfortable.

He smirked and placed his textbook down on the table. "How do you know I'm not trying to get ahead on the paper that's due..." He looked up at the ceiling, scrunching his eyebrows as though in deep thought. "In a month?"

"Because no one starts papers that far in advance." I shook my head and laughed. "Unless they're super uptight about school, and you don't seem like you are." I looked around the library to make sure no one was close enough to hear us, and lowered my voice. "Plus, why spend so much time studying when we can put an energy boost into our drinks and get our work done in double-time?"

"Or quadruple-time if we're talking about you," he said, holding my gaze. "Speaking of energy boosts in drinks, what happened in homeroom this morning?"

He certainly knew how to get to the point. And with Blake, I was quickly learning what that point always was—to get information about my abilities. He loved power.

And apparently I was bursting with it.

"I have no idea." I shook my head, my thoughts

returning to the prophecy. Maybe I should show it to Blake and get his opinion. After all, he'd shown me his secret with the fire. Which meant he owed it to me to keep my secret about this.

I took out the paper and placed it on the table. "Darius gave me this," I told him, scanning over the short paragraph again. "He says it's a prophecy. A girl in Kinsley wrote it more than three hundred years ago, and Darius thinks I can figure out what it means. So far I haven't had any luck."

Blake read it over, scrunching his eyebrows as he soaked it in. "What's an aether?" he asked, rubbing the back of his neck as he read it again.

"I don't know." I shrugged. "The whole thing makes no sense."

"So let's look it up." He pulled out his phone, and I rolled my eyes, feeling like an idiot for not thinking of doing online research myself. I guess I'd thought the answers would come to me, like magic.

He opened the web browser and typed "Aether" into the search engine. The first link that showed up led to the global encyclopedia. He clicked it, and the entry was huge.

"It says here that aether's the fifth element, also called spirit, and it's thought to be heavenly and not of the material world," he read out loud. He picked up the paper and held it next to his phone, as if trying to connect the information. "The prophecy says 'five representing each part of the world. That sounds like it could be related."

I took the phone and scrolled through the entry. A

circular diagram listed all of the elements, each in a different color. "Air, fire, earth, and water," I said, "with aether in the middle." I stared at it for a few more seconds, the pieces coming together. "There are five elements, and five of us were in the group under the comet. You can control fire. Danielle might be water. Kate mentioned something about her plants in biology growing more than they should have—maybe she's earth. Then there's Chris and me. I haven't noticed anything about the air, but maybe Chris and I are either air or aether."

"The prophecy could mean that something happened on the night of the comet to set this all into motion," Blake continued, scrolling down and reading more. "Which would make sense, since I didn't get my power over fire until after the comet."

I picked up the paper and re-read the prophecy. "So some sort of wall grew thin when the comet passed through the sky, our powers were ignited, and we need to restore the balance. But that still makes no sense. What does it mean that a wall is growing thin? And what sort of 'balance?'"

"I don't know." He sat back in his chair and scanned the page again, his brow wrinkled in thought.

"The five of us need to meet," I decided. "Because if we're right, it looks like we're going to have to work together in order to 'restore the balance'—whatever that means. We have to tell them about this as soon as possible so we can start brainstorming."

"Let's call them and meet at my house tonight," he said. "It's time we figure out some answers."

CHAPTER SEVENTEEN

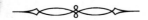

Kate and I walked up to Blake's house in silence. She'd been quieter than usual since I'd updated her during the car ride about the prophecy and what Blake and I had discussed. She didn't even mention the cut on my arm that she saw this morning before I healed it. Maybe she was waiting for me to bring it up first. Which I did plan on doing, once the group was together.

Blake's house was on top of a hill, Tudor style with gray and white bricks. It was bigger than most of the others on the street—including Danielle's. The wooden double door entrance was huge, the arch overhead reminding me of a palace.

He opened the door soon after we rang the bell.

"We're meeting in my room," he said, stepping aside to let us in. "Chris and Danielle are already here."

I walked through the doors and gazed around in awe. The wooden floors and antique furniture made me feel like I'd stepped into an old movie. A golden chandelier hung overhead, so extravagant that it felt like it should have been in an opera house instead of a foyer. Blake led us down the hall and through the kitchen, which looked like something out of a luxury design magazine. But we didn't get to see much of the house, because he opened a door leading to the basement and motioned us to go ahead.

"Your bedroom's in the basement?" I asked, glancing down the steps.

"I moved down here at the start of freshman year because it's more private," he said simply. "The basement is like my own little house."

I reached the bottom of the stairs, looked around, and what he'd said immediately made sense. A large open space held a ping-pong table, a foosball table, two pinball machines, and a small kitchen. We followed him further back into a white-carpeted living room area. Chris and Danielle were already there, the two of them on opposite sides of a wraparound sofa that faced a huge television.

Chris leaned back into the couch, his feet resting on the ottoman and his hands clasped behind his head. His gray t-shirt said Montgomery Biscuits in huge font, and the logo was cute—a smiling biscuit with a pad of butter for its tongue. Danielle was decked out in black leather pants and a silk strappy top. She looked ready for a party—not to hang out in a basement.

"Finally you're here," she said, studying her nails. "Blake told us about the ... thing that Darius showed you."

"You mean the prophecy?" I pulled the folded piece of paper out of my back pocket and waved it in the air.

She rolled her eyes. "Yeah, that."

Blake sat down next to her, and she placed her hand in his, a smug smile crossing her face. He didn't lean into her, but he didn't back away, either. He also refused to meet my eyes.

"So," I said, sitting as far away from Blake and Danielle as possible. "What do you all know so far?"

Chris jumped right in. "Blake's got some crazy fire power, Danielle just told us that she can control water, Kate makes plants grow without meaning to, and you made that glass explode today. And some prophecy talks about the comet making a wall grow thin, five representing each part of the world, and a journey east. I wouldn't mind a trip to Europe, but it makes no sense."

"That's the gist of it," I said, placing the paper on the coffee table and flattening out the creases.

Chris brought his hand up to his mouth and chewed his thumbnail. "So you all have cool powers, and I have nothing," he said. "That kind of blows."

"Maybe you have power over the air," I suggested. He stared at me blankly, and I continued, "You could try testing it out."

"And how should I do that?" The sarcasm in his tone surprised me. "Since you're apparently the expert on all of this, even though you've only been here for a little over a week."

"Chill out." Blake clenched his jaw and glared at Chris. "We won't figure anything out if we attack each other."

My heart leaped at Blake's defense of me. But when I tried to catch his gaze, he avoided me again, and I quickly deflated. So I looked away from him and focused on Chris. "Let's see if you have an ability that you didn't have before," I suggested. "Try doing something with air control."

"Air control?" He laughed and pushed his sleeves up to his elbows. "What does that even mean?"

"Try harnessing the air to create wind, and blow this paper off the table."

"Seriously?" He widened his eyes, looking at me like I'd lost my mind. "No one can do that. Not even the Elders."

"The Elders also can't control fire, water, and plants, or make glasses explode," Kate said from her spot on the floor. "You should try it. It's no more far-fetched than what any of us can do."

"Nicole's the one who made the glass explode," he said. "Couldn't that mean *she's* air?"

"It could," I said. "But what I did was ... different. I'll explain soon. First, it'll help if you try this. Please?"

He sat straighter and planted both feet on the floor. "All right," he said, leaning forward and rubbing his hands together. "Here goes nothing." He stared at the paper and narrowed his eyes, his forehead creased in concentration.

For a few seconds, nothing happened. Was I wrong in thinking he could do this? But then a gust of wind blew the paper off the table and across the room. It whirled up to slap the ceiling, and then fluttered to the floor next to the television.

"I did it!" Chris exclaimed, pumping his fist in the air. The paper swirled up again and landed back onto the table. "That was awesome." He fell back down on the couch and gave Kate a high five. She tucked her hair behind her ears and looked back down at the floor, a small smile on her face.

"Now, we know that you four each have control over a different element," I said, clasping my hands in my lap and looking at each of them. "It could relate to where the prophecy says, 'five representing each part of the world.'"

"Each element has a color it correlates to," Blake broke in. "Nicole and I looked it up online after Darius showed her the prophecy. Earth is green, fire is red, water is blue, and air is yellow."

Danielle huffed and crossed her arms. "Now we're basing our ideas off of Google searches." She rolled her eyes, her upper lip curled. "Great."

"Do you have any better ideas?" I asked.

"Not ideas, but I do have a question," she said. "If what you and Blake are saying is correct, then what does that make you? This says there are 'five representing each part of the world,' but there are only four elements."

"There are actually five elements, and I think Nicole is the final one," Blake spoke up again. "Aether. It also means spirit, or power of life. The prophecy says 'the Aether will ignite them,' so 'them' must be the four other elements—the elements we can control. Under the comet we felt an electric shock. That could have been when our new powers manifested."

"So the comet gave us these powers," Chris said. "And it was ignited by the Aether. Which is you." He pointed at me, his eyes serious. "But have you been able to use 'the spirit of life'—whatever that means?"

I looked around at all of them and took a deep breath. It was now or never. "You all saw what happened in homeroom this morning—when the glass broke?" I asked.

Everyone nodded, which I took as a sign to continue. Even Danielle crossed her legs and faced my direction, looking mildly interested in what I had to say.

"A shard of the glass got into my arm," I said, glancing down at my wrist. "I panicked and took it out, and when I was putting pressure on it to stop the bleeding, I imagined it healing." I held my hand over the same spot on my arm, remembering how easy it had been to fix. "It worked."

Danielle uncrossed her legs and placed her hands on her knees. "Let me get this straight," she said. "You healed a gash on your arm in less than a minute?"

"I don't know how long it took..."

"It was about ten seconds," Kate said.

"Okay." I smiled at her in thanks and turned back to Danielle. "Ten seconds. That could be what 'the spirit of life' means—the power to heal."

Danielle nodded and sat back in the couch. If I didn't know any better, I might have thought she was impressed. By *me*.

"So we've gone over most of the prophecy," Blake said quickly. "But we haven't talked about the last line—the one about the Journey and the Shadows. Do any of you have an idea about what it could mean?"

"No clue." I shrugged and looked around to see if anyone else had an idea. No one spoke up.

"I'm as stumped as the rest of you," Chris said after a few long seconds. "And I'm also hungry. Why don't we go to Sophie's and talk about it there? Maybe a change of scenery will help us think."

I looked at him and tilted my head. "Who's Sophie?" I asked.

"Sophie's Diner." He laughed. "Open 24 hours, got the best food around."

My stomach growled with the thought. "I haven't been there yet," I told him. "And food does sound amazing right now."

"Then we definitely have to go." He stood up and headed towards the stairs before anyone could disagree, and we piled into our cars to head to Sophie's Diner, which Chris swore had the best burgers in the state of Massachusetts.

CHAPTER EIGHTEEN

The delicious smell of greasy food filled my nose the second I walked inside Sophie's Diner, making my mouth water. The sea foam green booths looked welcoming, and the mini-jukeboxes on the walls gave the place a fun fifties vibe. Even though I hadn't tried the food yet, I already loved it here.

"Table for five?" the hostess asked, grabbing menus from the stack on the stand.

"A booth would be great," Blake said smoothly.

We followed her to a booth in the corner, which wrapped around in a semi-circle, and got ourselves situated. The menu had tons of options, but I ultimately went with a burger, since Chris said they were the best.

The waitress brought our drinks out first. The hot chocolate smelled amazing, and I took a sip without bothering to test how hot it was. It scorched my tongue, and I gasped and chugged some water, hoping I hadn't temporarily destroyed my taste buds.

Without asking if I minded, Danielle reached across the table and wrapped her hand around my steaming mug. I almost yanked it out of her grip, but stopped when I saw how intensely she was staring at it.

Finally, she pulled her hand back and looked at me. "Try it now," she said simply.

I hesitated. Hopefully she hadn't poisoned my drink with gray energy. However, doubting she would do that with everyone watching, I lifted the mug and took a sip, preparing to burn my tongue for a second time.

The hot chocolate was the perfect temperature.

"How did you do that?" I asked, placing it back down.

"My element is water," she said. "Obviously there's water in hot chocolate, so I gathered blue energy and thought about the drink cooling off. I guess it worked."

"Cool!" Chris placed both palms on the table, his eyes lighting up. "Can you boil my water?"

"Not unless you want me to melt the plastic." Danielle laughed, looking at him like he was a few brain cells short. "Although I might be able to do this." She reached forward and wrapped her hand around his cup, the same intense expression in her eyes that she'd had when cooling my hot chocolate.

The ice cubes in Chris's water melted in seconds.

"Wow." Chris's mouth dropped open. "Impressive."

"But not exceptionally useful," she said, dropping her arm back to her side. "I'm going to figure out some more things I can do with it later."

It was tempting to say something along the lines of "besides making water fountains explode in peoples faces," but I held back. There was no need to start an unnecessary argument now.

"Good plan," I said instead, taking another sip of hot chocolate.

"So, why are Journey and Shadows capitalized in the prophecy?" Chris asked after we got our food.

"I've been thinking about that," Kate said. "In standard English, only proper nouns are capitalized. So the capitalized words could represent names or locations."

"Thanks for the grammar lesson," Danielle said, grabbing a packet of fake sugar and dumping it into her coffee.

I ignored her and re-focused on the prophecy. "So we have to go on a Journey down a path to ... the Shadows." I paused to take a bite of my burger, and to think. What could that *mean*? It still didn't make any sense.

We sat in silence, eating our food and trying to come up with ideas. Everyone else seemed to be drawing a blank, too.

"Sophie!" Chris yelled, waving his arms in the air and zapping me out of my thoughts. "Hey."

A large woman with a huge, toothy smile walked towards us. She looked about my grandmother's age, with wrinkly skin and a few brown spots on her face.

Her gray hair was pulled into a tight bun at the nape of her neck, and she wore a long blue dress that made her look like she'd stepped right out of an old village.

"Chris," she greeted him. "It's good to see you again. It's been ... two days?"

"I can't resist the burgers," he said with a laugh. "Plus Nicole just moved here, and we all know that eating at Sophie's is a must in Kinsley."

"Nicole." Sophie looked at me and smiled. "Victory of the people."

"What?" I scrunched my eyebrows and tilted my head.

"The origin of your name is Greek," she said. "It means 'victory of the people.'"

It was a strange thing to say, but I nodded, assuming she was just a quirky older lady. "Are you from Greece?" I asked.

"I was born there, yes," she replied. "I moved here with my family about thirty years ago, and we opened the diner together. Been running it ever since."

"I've never known the town without Sophie's." Chris shook some hair out of his eyes and turned back to her. "Hey, maybe you can help us out with something. It's homework for our Greek mythology class."

I took a sharp breath inward, ready to stop him from showing her the prophecy. But maybe it wouldn't be bad to get an outsider's perspective. Sophie was from Greece, and we were descended from the Greek gods. She might be able to help.

"I can try," Sophie said. "But not for long. I do have other customers to tend to." She winked, and even though the diner was packed, it looked like there was enough staff to handle it.

Chris passed the paper to her. "We're trying to figure out what this means," he said. "We think we have the beginning figured out, but the last sentence has us stumped. Do you have any idea why Journey and Shadows would be capitalized?"

Her eyes turned serious as she read it over. "I have no idea what most of this means," she mused, holding a chubby finger to her chin. "But 'journey' translates to odyssey in Greek—like the book. The name Odessa, like Odessa Road, stems from that word."

"The main street in town..." I said, the pieces starting to fall into place.

"It's just an idea." She shrugged and handed the prophecy back to Chris. "But I've got to get back to work. Good luck on the homework." She turned and headed to another table, not giving us a chance to ask any more questions.

I grabbed the ketchup and squirted a large amount onto my plate. "If Sophie's right, then we need to go east on Odessa Road," I said, dipping a fry into the ketchup and eating it. "It sounds like a long shot, but it's all we've got."

"You really think an ancient prophecy is talking about a street in *Kinsley*?" Danielle sneered. "That makes no sense."

"The prophecy was written three hundred years ago, which doesn't make it 'ancient,'" Blake pointed out. "Kinsley's been around for longer than that. And Odessa's one of the oldest roads in town. So it's possible."

Danielle huffed, stabbed a piece of lettuce with her fork, and popped it in her mouth. Blake imitated her by doing the same thing with his ravioli, but ten times more exaggerated. She glared at him and continued eating, although she stopped stabbing her food.

They were so familiar with each other. Who was I to think that Blake might be interested in me—someone he'd only known for a *week*? He was interested in my abilities—not in me. The sooner I accepted that, the sooner I could focus on the things that mattered. Like the prophecy and learning how to use my new powers.

"So we have an idea about what Journey could mean," I said, picking up the paper and skimming it again. "But what about Shadows?"

"It sounds foreboding." Chris laughed and finished his last fry.

"It does," I agreed. "Maybe we should just go east and see what happens."

Danielle rolled her eyes. "What a solid plan."

I dropped the prophecy on the table and sat back in the booth. "Do you have any better ideas?" I asked.

She scowled and concentrated on eating her salad, which I guessed was a no.

"Should we get started on this 'journey' now?" Blake broke the silence.

I looked out the window, the sight of the night sky sending a sinking feeling through my stomach. Without the sun shining overhead I felt ... unprotected.

"It's late," I said, glancing at my watch. 10:30 pm. "I

have a midnight curfew. So we should wait until tomorrow and go during the day. We'll have more time, and we'll be able to see better."

"Are you afraid of the dark?" Chris raised his hands into makeshift claws, wiggling his fingers in my face. "The scary creatures of the night are going to get you!"

"I'm not afraid of the dark." I swatted his hand away, laughing. "It just seems like a better plan."

"We should listen to Nicole," Kate said, so serious that we stopped laughing. "She's had good instincts so far."

"I say we go now," Danielle argued. "I can't imagine that a drive down Odessa Road will take longer than an hour. If it does, we'll stop so you can get home in time and resume tomorrow. It'll be more efficient."

"Maybe." I looked out the window again and shivered. "I don't know. It's hard to explain, but I feel stronger during the day. Do any of you feel that way, too?"

A few seconds passed in silence.

"Not really," Blake finally said. "But I'll trust you on that."

"We should vote," Kate suggested. "Who wants to go tomorrow?"

She put her hand up, followed by Chris's, mine, and eventually Blake's. The unsettled feeling in my body calmed down. The majority of the group trusted my instincts. And I couldn't help but smile at how Blake had taken my side over Danielle's.

"Four to one," Chris said triumphantly. "We go tomorrow morning. Let's meet back here at ten. The sun will be high in the sky, and we'll need some breakfast before our perilous journey."

"Perilous journey?" I repeated, arching an eyebrow.

He shrugged. "It sounds more adventurous."

While I agreed with him, I hoped the journey wasn't as dangerous as he'd made it sound—or at least not so dangerous that someone would end up getting hurt.

CHAPTER NINETEEN

Falling asleep that night was impossible.

My mind buzzed with everything that had happened since my first day at Kinsley High—learning I'm a witch, seeing the comet, reading the prophecy, and knowing that tomorrow I would embark on a journey that may or may not be dangerous.

I was staring at the ceiling with a million thoughts running through my mind when my cell phone dinged with a text.

Are you up?

It was from Blake. I read it a few more times, my fingers hovering over the keys. What should I text back? *Should* I text back at all? I'd already resigned myself to the fact that nothing was going to happen between us. Replying now, so late at night, would just blur those lines and give me hope. Hope that I shouldn't *want* to have.

It would be easiest to ignore the text until tomorrow and pretend like I'd been sleeping when he'd sent it. That way, no one would get hurt.

But if I didn't reply, I would toss and turn all night, unable to fall asleep because I would be so curious about what he wanted to say.

So I *had* to text him back. It would drive me too crazy if I didn't.

Yeah, I typed. *I'm trying to sleep, but it's not working well.*

I sent it, and his response came in seconds.

Wanna hang out? I can come pick you up.

My heart jumped into my throat. Because yes, of course I wanted to hang out with Blake. I wanted to see him—just the two of us, alone—more than anything. I wanted to know if whatever I was feeling for him was just in my head, or if he felt it, too. Because if he was reaching out to me like this, it had to mean he was interested. Right?

Unfortunately, it wasn't that simple, no matter how much I wished it could be.

What about your girlfriend? I asked.

I watched the text bubble move as he typed, so nervous that I could barely breathe.

Things with Danielle are ... complicated. It's too much to explain over text.

Hope rose in my chest, and despite knowing that "complicated" didn't mean they were broken up, now I definitely wanted to see him. I needed to know the full story.

Of course, to see him I would have to sneak out, which I'd never done before. But my parents were sound sleepers and had been in bed for hours. They would never know I'd left. And if they did catch me, I could always put blue energy into their morning coffee so they would be calm and relaxed about it tomorrow.

Sure. I typed quickly so I couldn't overthink what I was doing. I didn't want time to talk myself out of this. *I'm on 404 Cypress Street.*

I kept my phone in my hand while I waited for him to reply, staring anxiously at the screen.

Be there in 10.

I dropped the phone on my bed and got up to change out of my pajamas. As I decided on an outfit, I couldn't help second-guessing my decision to see him. He had a girlfriend. And despite things being "complicated" between them, I would bet that Danielle would be pretty angry if she found out that Blake had texted me to hang out tonight.

At the same time, I wanted to learn about whatever this "complication" was. Seeing him tonight didn't mean that anything was going to happen between us.

Of course, this was under the assumption that he was interested in me at all. Maybe he really couldn't sleep and wanted a friend to spend time with, and I was the only one awake. Or worse—maybe he wanted to ask me for advice on his relationship with Danielle.

Not wanting to over-analyze the situation, I returned my attention to getting ready. As I dabbed on concealer, I noticed that the dark circles under my eyes were terrible. In addition to the lack of sleep, the stress of everything I'd found out recently must have been getting to me more than I'd realized.

Once ready, I paced around my room, waiting for Blake to text me that he was here. Finally my phone buzzed.

I'm in front of your house … I think. Blue with the gabled windows?

I peeked through the blinds. A black Range Rover was parked on the street, with Blake in the driver's seat.

I see you, I wrote back. *I'll be out in a minute.*

I walked out of my room and into the hall. My parents' room was on the first floor, so the second floor of the house was small—only the bathroom and the steps separated my room from my sister's. Light shined from underneath her door, and I heard the tapping of computer keys as she talked with her friends online.

I hadn't expected her to still be awake. This would make things trickier.

My door creaked loudly as it closed—stupid old houses. I only made it one more step before Becca's door opened.

She crossed her arms and leaned against the wall, a smug smile on her face. "Where are you off to right now?" she asked, glancing up and down at my outfit.

"Nowhere." My voice shook, and I placed a hand on the top of the railing.

"Come on." She brought her dark, curly hair in

front of her shoulders and combed her fingers through it. "You're totally sneaking out."

"No, I'm not," I said, although I sounded far from convincing. "I was just going downstairs to get a snack."

"And that required you to get dressed and put on makeup?" She smirked and raised an eyebrow. "Just because I'm younger than you doesn't mean I'm stupid."

"I know that," I said. "I never said you were."

"Then stop lying to me." She pouted and leaned against the doorframe. "Because all I'm wondering is … who are you going to see?"

Relief flooded my chest at how she sounded amused by the situation, and not like she wanted to stop me. "A friend from school," I said quickly, hoping I wasn't taking so long that Blake thought I was standing him up. "Don't tell Mom and Dad, okay?"

"Fine." She rolled her eyes. "But you owe me." She stomped to the bathroom and shut the door, closing it with more force than necessary.

I made it downstairs and out of the house without any more trouble. The front door shut quietly, and I took a deep breath before walking towards Blake's Range Rover. I couldn't believe he was here, and that I was actually doing this.

Trying to will my hands to stop shaking, I opened the door and slid into the passenger seat, smiling in a way that I hoped looked casual. "Hi," I said softly, keeping my eyes locked on his as I clicked my seatbelt into place. His hair was a bit messy, and he also had circles under his eyes. But he managed to pull it off so he looked more like a rock star than a sleep deprived teen.

"Hey." His voice was smooth, and he smiled in a way that made me believe he was truly happy I'd come out. "You look good for not being able to sleep."

"Thanks. So do you." My cheeks heated, and I glanced down at my hands. I wanted more than anything to ask him about Danielle, but I didn't want to push it too quickly. "Where are we going?" I asked instead.

"There's an old playground at the Hemlock Center." He put the car into drive and headed down my street. "We could go there and hang out."

"What's the Hemlock Center?" I asked.

"It used to be a house, but the state bought the property and changed it into a school in the early 1900's. It was a school for people with ... behavior problems, you could say."

"Like an institution?"

"Exactly." He nodded, his gaze fixed on the road. "But it closed a few years ago because of problems with safety codes. Now it's just a bunch of abandoned buildings."

I eyed him cautiously. "And you go there to hang out a lot?"

"I used to with friends," he said. "Usually it's used by freshmen who want a private place to drink. It's late enough now that it should be quiet."

I nodded and looked out the window. There were practically no cars on the road at this time of night.

Most people were asleep—like I should have been.

Then again, most people weren't worried about fulfilling a possibly dangerous prophecy tomorrow.

Blake turned onto a dark winding road, and I spotted a three-story stone building with large white columns. The roof had a sharp slant, like the Haunted Mansions in theme parks, with gabled windows on the third floor. A bare tree curved around the side, its looming branches standing guard against unwanted visitors.

He parked the car near a sprawling wooden playground, and I brightened when I saw it. Now I understood why he wanted to come here. The playground must have had ten small platforms on all different levels, some bigger than others. The highest ones had roofs in the shape of fairy-tale towers. Narrow steps and bridges connected each platform to the next. Each platform had different ways of getting onto them—logs, ladders, tires, steps—and the one on the furthest end led out to a set of wooden monkey bars. It reminded me of the Robinson Treehouse.

Nearby was an old merry-go-round—metal, with bars to hold onto, and a thick pole in the center. It looked like it had been built in a different decade than the rest of the playground.

I walked to the merry-go-round, skimming my hand along the rail. Blake followed close behind. "I haven't been on one of these since fourth grade," I said, smiling at the memory. "I fell off the side from trying to make it spin too fast."

"I can picture that." He laughed. "This time, how

about I spin it and you stay in the center so you don't fall off?"

I tilted my head, like I was unsure, even though there wasn't a chance I would say no. "Okay," I finally said. "But if I do fall, it's your fault for talking me into it." I climbed onto it and smiled at him, tossing my hair over my shoulders and situating myself in the center.

"I won't let you fall." He grabbed the outside rail and started to run before I could say anything more. The playground and the surrounding buildings blurred around me, and it was like I was back in elementary school enjoying recess with my friends. My hair flew in all directions, and even though the wind rushed past my face, the cold didn't bother me. I laughed and looked up at the stars spinning overhead, shining in the cloudless night. They looked like sparkling diamonds.

Blake jumped on to join me, sitting so close that his arm brushed against mine. Even though we were both wearing jackets, my skin tingled at the proximity to his. We admired the stars in silence, and the merry-go-round spun slower and slower, creaking a few times before going still.

"For a moment I forgot about the prophecy and what we're doing tomorrow," I said, running my hands through my hair in an attempt to untangle it. "It all seems so surreal."

His eyes filled with intensity, and he leaned closer, leaving barely any space between us. "Everything's been that way since you moved to town," he said.

"Surreal."

My breath caught, and I was trapped in his gaze. "What do you mean by that?" I asked.

"Nothing's been normal since you got here," he said. "After all, if you weren't here, I might not be able to do this." He took out his lighter and flicked it on, shooting a fireball into an arc above our heads. It looked like a meteor, dying out before reaching the ground. Then he shot up four more. The sparks of light reminded me of a fountain show, but with fire instead of water.

I watched until they went out, amazed that all of this was real. My world had gone from normal to magical in only a few days. Everything I'd once believed to be true had been turned upside down, and even though it was crazy and possibly dangerous, I loved every second of it.

"I just don't understand why my powers are different than everyone else's," I confessed what had been keeping me up all night. "You and the others can control the elements. That seems more useful than what I can do."

"Maybe it's because spirit is so different from the physical elements," he said. "But I think your power could be the most useful of them all. I actually wanted to try something with it." He pulled out a pocketknife, and before I could ask him what he was doing, he pushed back the sleeve of his jacket, lowered the blade to his arm, and made a small incision. A thin line of blood emerged from the cut, bright red against his skin.

"Why did you *do* that?" I asked, looking from the cut

to his face and back again.

"So you can practice using your power," he said. "I would never ask you to do that to yourself, so I had to do it to me." He held his arm out and watched me expectantly. "Now—are you going to heal this or what?"

"Of course I'll try." I rested my hand over the cut, his blood sticky against my palm. "But I've only done this once, and I had no idea what I was doing. I'm sorry if it doesn't work again."

"It'll work," he said. "I believe in you."

I wished I believed in myself half as much as he apparently believed in me. But since I didn't want to leave him bleeding for any longer than necessary, I closed my eyes and tried to recreate whatever I'd done when I healed my own arm in class. I pictured white energy flowing through my body, feeling the warm tingle as it rushed through my arm and came out of my palm. Once the energy died out, I opened my eyes and lifted my hand.

The cut was still there. I watched, defeated, as a drop of his blood leaked out and dripped onto the floor of the merry-go-round.

Apparently I wasn't as powerful as Blake thought I was. He'd had so much faith in me that he'd *injured* himself, and I couldn't even heal him. I was a failure.

"Try to imagine what the cut feels like." He leaned closer, his forehead nearly touching mine, and my heart pounded faster. "Think about when you healed yourself. You did it before, so you can do it now. I know it."

"Okay." I closed my eyes and imagined the cut on my arm instead of on his, transferring whatever pain he was feeling onto myself. Calling forth the white energy again, I allowed it to flow out of my palm where my hand rested on his arm, picturing the skin knitting together and returning to normal. At the same time I felt the same thing happening to me, until the pain I'd created in my mind disappeared and the last bit of white energy flowed out of my body. Then I opened my eyes to see if it worked.

His skin was smooth, as though the cut had never existed in the first place.

"Perfect." He nodded and pulled his sleeve back down. "Now if any of us get injured, we know you can fix it."

"I don't know how much I can do," I said, leaning back against the pole to stop my head from spinning. "It wears me out pretty fast."

"It'll get easier with practice," he assured me. "The same way that athletes get stronger the more they work out."

"It works the same way for us?"

"It's why the Elders are so powerful," he said. "But I have a feeling that it'll come naturally to you. There's something different about your powers—something I've never seen before. You shouldn't have been able to *capture* energy on your first day, and now, a week later, you have that mastered *and* you're healing people. It's incredible."

"There's something different about *all* of our powers," I reminded him. "Me, you, Kate, Chris, and

Danielle."

"True," he said. "So I guess none of us know what to expect now."

We stared at the stars again, the mention of Danielle's name hanging in the air. I couldn't put off asking about her any longer.

"What did you mean in your text?" I asked, needing to get the question off my chest. "When you said that things were complicated between you and Danielle?"

"I'm surprised it took you so long to ask," he said, and I leaned forward, waiting for him to continue. "Things between me and Danielle ... haven't been great recently. I don't know how much you know, so I'm just going to put it out there—there's a group of us that get together privately to practice using gray energy. It's not illegal, but we're not taught it in school, so we wanted to train ourselves to use it. We never thought we would need it, but teaching ourselves something we're not allowed to learn in school was fun. Then, last semester, Danielle started using it on humans. At first it was small things, like putting gray energy into the pens of people she didn't like right before they took a test, so they would mess up."

"And putting gray energy into my tennis racket?" I asked.

"Exactly," he said. "But then, in November, she put gray energy into a girl's drink, just because the girl was talking to me at a party."

"Were you ... interested in that girl?" I didn't want to accuse him of anything, but I was curious if Danielle had an actual reason to be jealous. It wouldn't make what she did okay, but I still wanted to know.

"No," he said immediately. "Not at all. We had woodworking together, and we were talking about our latest project for class. She was shy and seemed uncomfortable at the party, so I didn't want to leave her by herself. Then Danielle saw us, jumped to conclusions, and put gray energy into her drink right before she drove home ..." He paused and looked out at the trees, his eyes pained at the memory.

"Kate told me about what happened to her." I reached for him and rested my hand on his arm, glad when he didn't move away. "I hope you know it's not your fault."

"It's Danielle's fault," he said, snapping back into focus. "And I haven't been able to look at her the same since."

"But you're still with her," I said. "Why?"

"I ended things with her right after it happened," he said. "She'd changed too much from the person she was when we'd first started dating, and I didn't like who she'd become. But she came crying to me a week later, promising she wouldn't use gray energy anymore, and begged me to give her another chance. So I did. But after what she pulled on you during your tennis try-out the other day, I'm done. She loves using gray energy too much to give it up, and I hate thinking that anyone I talk to is at risk of getting hurt by her. I was planning on telling her tonight, but then everything happened with the prophecy, and I couldn't risk it. Because whatever we have to do tomorrow is important, and I have no idea *what* she'll do when I tell her it's over."

"Wow." I let out a long breath, and realizing how long my hand had been resting on his arm, I pulled it back onto my lap. "I had no idea. But thank you for telling me. For *trusting* me. It means a lot."

"And it means a lot to me that you gave me a chance tonight and heard me out," he said. "Danielle's so jealous of you—I'm worried that after I end it with her, she'll blame you. And I don't want her to do anything that might hurt you."

"I have you, Kate, and Chris on my side," I said. "The three of you will protect me. And I have ways to protect myself now, too."

"True." He smiled. "You do."

"But Danielle's so confident and strong," I said. "Why would she be jealous of *me*?"

"Let's see..." He leaned back and looked up at the stars, as if he had as many reasons as the lights twinkling up above. "You're more powerful than her. You're better at tennis. Your element—the aether—is the center of all of ours. You're the one who Darius entrusted with the prophecy. And using your powers is so natural to you that it seems like you have more potential than any of us. It's impressive." He smiled at me, and my stomach did that whole flipping thing again.

Hopefully the cold air disguised the redness creeping onto my cheeks. "Thanks," I said softly, glancing down at my hands.

"I mean it," he said, scooting closer to me. I shivered, unsure if it was because of the wind or the fact that Blake's hand brushed softly against mine. "Still not used to the cold?" he asked.

"I don't think I'll ever get used to it," I said. "Especially at night. Not that the night isn't pretty, but it's warmer during the day. I love being in the sun."

"So let's create our own sun." He flicked on the lighter and grabbed the flame, floating it above his palm. It grew into a yellow sphere the size of a snow globe, and the heat warmed my face, stopping my shivering. The fire had taken on a life of its own.

He put the lighter back in his pocket and held his other hand underneath the fire as well, balancing the orb of light in his palms. It grew to the size of a basketball and floated up until it was right above our heads.

He'd created our own personal sun.

"Wow." I stared up at it in amazement. "That's incredible."

"Thanks," he said. "I've been practicing."

He was watching me so intensely, and I wondered if he was about to kiss me. My heart fluttered at the thought. I'd never been kissed before—that one time during truth or dare at tennis camp last summer didn't count—and I didn't know what to expect. All I knew was that I wanted this—I wanted *him*.

But just when he started moving closer, a twig snapped behind us, and I glanced over my shoulder to see what it was.

"Is someone there?" I whispered, panic flooding my veins. Were we even allowed to be here right now? What if the cops found us and were going to get us in trouble? Hopefully they wouldn't call my parents. I would definitely be grounded if my parents found out that I'd snuck out *and* had gotten caught for breaking and entering. Well, we hadn't *broken* anything, but we did *enter*.

"It's probably an animal." Blake looked back up at the fire and made it burn brighter. "They're everywhere around here."

Just as he said it, something growled and stepped out of the shadows. At first I thought it was a wolf, but whatever this ... creature was, it definitely wasn't something I'd heard of before. It looked like a science experiment gone horribly wrong. Its neck was split into two, each one sprouting a separate head. Its tail stood on end—a scaly thing that looked like it belonged on a scorpion, the spiky tip pointing straight into the air.

I grabbed Blake's arm and looked at him to check if he was seeing this, too. Judging by the horror splashed across his face, he was.

Growling again, the creature dug its front claws into the dirt and lowered its heads to the ground, its glowing yellow eyes locked on ours.

Then it chomped its teeth together, let out a feral growl, and charged.

CHAPTER TWENTY

"Run!" Blake yelled, grabbing my arm and pulling me off of the merry-go-round.

It spun under our weight, and I held onto the metal bars, pushing off them to leap over the edge. The cedar chips on the ground cushioned my landing. The car was behind us, which would mean running towards the monstrous hound, so I bolted for the playground, hurrying up a ladder of rubber tires that led to the closest platform. Blake followed close behind. The second he was up he took the lighter out of his pocket and aimed a blue fireball at the tires, melting them to the ground seconds before the hound reached them.

It looked up at us and growled—a low, menacing sound that if I spoke dog I would have assumed meant

"I'm going to have you for dinner"—and tried to jump onto the platform. It missed by only a few inches.

Blake flicked on his lighter and threw a fireball at the hound's chest, but it jumped to the side to get out of the way. It turned all four of its eyes up at us, one head letting out a deep roar as the other snapped its teeth together, taking bites out of the air.

My hands shook, and I gripped one of the log posts behind me for support. "Have you learned how to fight these things in homeroom?" I asked Blake, my voice rising in panic.

He threw another fireball, and it missed the hound again. "No," he snapped, the flames lighting up his face. "Fighting legendary creatures isn't on the syllabus."

"Maybe it should be," I said as he launched another ball of fire, hitting the hound on its front paw. Both of its heads yelped in pain. The scorpion tail lowered between its legs, and it growled again before turning away from us and running around the side of the playground, woodchips flying behind it as it gained speed.

My heart pounded, and I looked around to figure how to get off the platform. The exit was a slide that dropped off at the monkey bars. I could get down and run to the car, but I didn't know where the hound was, and leaving the platform could give it the perfect opportunity to pounce.

Then the hound growled again. I turned around, spotting it clamoring up a ladder of logs that led to a nearby platform. Only a wobbly bridge separated that platform from our own. My entire body shook, and I moved closer to Blake, grabbing his arm for support.

The hound reached the top of the platform, and its glowing eyes narrowed, ready to attack.

Not having anywhere else to go, I launched myself down the slide and hurried to the monkey bars, climbing up the ladder and hoisting myself on top of them. Gripping the sides, I crawled to the center bar, but the ground spun beneath me, my lungs tightening as I looked down. I had to take a few deep breaths to steady myself. A six-foot fall wasn't deadly. Now wasn't the time to let my fear of heights get to me.

Blake scrambled behind me, and I turned around to make sure he wasn't hurt. Sweat dripped down the sides of his face from the flames, but other than that he looked okay. He took his lighter out again, holding it up in preparation to create another fireball.

I looked back at the hound in time to see it run along the bridge and hurl itself towards us. It bared its teeth as it flew through the air, its arms outstretched as it came closer to the monkey bars. But it must not have had enough force behind the jump, because it fell to the ground with a loud thump. It stood and shook the woodchips off its fur, a low growl coming from somewhere deep in its throat as it turned its heads up to look at us.

Before I could say anything to Blake about how completely screwed we were, he threw two balls of fire towards the hound, hitting both of its faces. It howled and collapsed, whimpering as it buried its snouts in its paws. The smell of burnt skin filled the air. My stomach swirled with nausea, and I lifted a hand to my nose to block out the odor.

Only a few seconds passed before it stood up again. The fur on its faces had changed into a charred grey. Its yellow eyes glowed brighter now, both snouts chomping madly in the air, strings of saliva dripping to the ground as it waited to devour whichever one of us lost our balance first.

Then I had a crazy idea.

"Can you burn the wood around one of these metal bars and get it out?" I pointed to show Blake what I meant. The poles to grab on to while swinging across the monkey bars were metal, but the rest of the structure was wood. If Blake could burn a small amount of wood away that surrounded one of the poles, the metal could come loose.

"Without the whole structure falling down?" He looked at me like I'd lost my mind. "If I can, what do you plan on doing with it ... using it as a sword?"

"Sort of," I said. "Unless you have a better idea? Because what we're doing now isn't working."

He examined a metal bar on the end, running his hands along the edges where it met with the wood. "I should be able to do it," he said, glancing down at the hound. It jumped in the air and snapped its teeth, only missing us by a foot. "But if the structure falls, run for it." He took his keys out of his pocket and placed them in my palm, wrapping my fist around them. "I'll distract it, and you get to the car. Don't wait for me."

"You want me to leave you to deal with that thing alone?" Now I looked at *him* like he was crazy. "No way."

"I can hold it off with my power," he insisted. "I'll be fine."

The hound walked away before I could respond, not looking back as it disappeared behind the playground.

"Is it leaving?" I whispered.

Blake shook his head, his hand ready with his lighter. "I don't think so."

It reappeared in my line of sight, and I realized what it was doing. A few platforms away was another way up the jungle gym—a single log that looked like a large balance beam slanted upwards—and it was heading right towards it.

Blake must have realized what it was doing too, because he threw another ball of fire towards the hound. The flames hit the tip of its scorpion tail. The fire took only a few seconds to go out, and the hound jumped onto the platform we were on earlier, glaring at us. It backed up to the other end of the bridge and dug its legs into the wood like a bull about to attack.

I tightened my grip on the edges of the monkey bars. "Get me the metal bar," I said, my voice surprisingly steady considering that my heart was beating so fast that it felt like it was about to burst out of my chest. "Now."

He flicked on the lighter, directing the fire towards the wood around the farthest pole. I held on to the sides for support in case it collapsed, keeping watch on the hound. It must have known what we were doing, because it raced across the bridge, gaining speed in preparation to jump.

Blake yanked the bar out of the wood and handed it to me. My hand wrapped around the metal, and it was like time slowed down. The hound leaped off the platform and soared through the air, all four of its eyes on me. I zeroed in on my target—the spot on its chest where its heart should be—and my mind *knew* what to do. It was like looking through a high-tech sniper rifle. I could see exactly where to aim, and knew how much force I needed to use and what angle to point the pole to hit the moving target. It felt similar to when I evaluated how to hit a ball in tennis towards a specific spot on the court, only a million times more accurate, like the adrenaline coursing through my veins had set my mind on super-speed.

I pulled my arm back and sent the pole flying, directing it on a straight, smooth path exactly where I'd intended. It connected with the target, and two high-pitched yelps sounded through the air, followed by a bang as the hound collided with the ground.

Everything was silent for the first time since the hound had appeared. I leaned over the edge of the monkey bars to check on it, grimacing at what I saw. The pole had gotten stuck in its body, entering its chest and coming out through its back. Blood glistened on the metal. One of its heads twisted at an unnatural angle, and the other whimpered before closing its eyes and falling lifeless on the ground. Its tail twitched a few times and went still.

I almost felt bad for the thing—but then I remembered how it had tried to make Blake and me into a late-night snack, and I didn't feel quite as guilty.

Now was the issue of what to do with the body.

Before I could ask Blake for any ideas, the hound flickered like a faulty projected image and disappeared. All that remained was the pole, half-covered in blood.

I looked around, checking if there were any other monsters lurking in the darkness. Piles of woodchips crackled with flames, but other than that, nothing seemed to be moving.

"I think we can get down now," I said.

Blake headed towards the ladder, but when he shifted his weight, the monkey bars collapsed, dumping us onto the ground. My breath caught at the impact. I broke the fall with my elbows and knees, rolling over the woodchips and colliding with Blake.

He sat up and ran a hand through his hair, which had gotten messed up in the fall. "I guess the wood didn't take well to the fire." He chuckled, and we both looked around the playground to examine the damage. The monkey bars dangled from one end like someone had taken a chainsaw to the middle of them. The flames on the woodchips were growing taller, and they lit up portions of the jungle gym, threatening to burn it all down.

He held his hands up in the air and slowly lowered them. As he did, the fire receded until it was snuffed out completely.

I examined my palms, which were cut up from the woodchips. "At least falling off the monkey bars is better than..." I looked at the place where the hound had been, scrunching my nose at the bloody pole lying on the ground.

"Than being ripped to shreds by a two-headed scorpion-tailed dog-monster?" Blake finished my thought. "I definitely agree with you there."

CHAPTER TWENTY-ONE

My injuries weren't bad—only a few scratches—and I called on white energy to heal them. They disappeared in seconds. Blake had a few cuts too, so I healed him as well, but using the energy wore me out. My head felt like a lead weight, and I could barely keep my eyes open.

"You look tired," Blake said as we walked to the car. "Let's go back and get some sleep so we're ready for whatever we'll be up against tomorrow. We'll tell the others about what happened in the morning."

I nodded, glad when we reached the car so I could sit down. My mind felt hazy, and all I wanted was to close my eyes, lean against the window, and go to sleep.

Then I remembered something I wanted to ask him. I'd been hesitant to bring it up before because I didn't want to be intrusive, but one question couldn't hurt. Plus, we'd just had a bonding experience. It's not every day that you have to work together to fight off a mythological monster that wants to kill you.

"I heard that you and your friends don't like humans very much," I began, watching him in the hope that the question wasn't too personal. "Is that true?"

He stayed focused on the road, his jaw muscles tight. "It's not that we don't like them," he said simply. "But we *are* more powerful than humans. Is it so bad to see them as weak?"

"It's not their fault that they don't have powers," I said. "We're not any more deserving than they are. We didn't do anything special to be like this. It's just the way we were born."

"It's different when you've grown up knowing about what you can do," he said. "Humans are weak. We're powerful. Think of it like … natural selection."

I looked out the window, not wanting to hear any more. Because it just reminded me that Blake only liked me because of my powers. He wouldn't have noticed me at all if I were normal.

He pulled up in front of my house and turned to look at me. "Nicole," he said, the smoothness of his voice making my name sound like music. "I don't want you to take what I said about humans the wrong way. I'm not a bad person. I promise."

My thoughts drifted to the clay sun he'd made for

me in ceramics, and the time we'd spent together on the merry-go-round before getting attacked by the two-headed hound. "You just saved my *life* at the playground," I said. "No one's ever done anything like that for me before. I could never think you were a bad person."

"Good." He reached forward and brushed his fingers against my hand, sending a surge of heat up my arm. "I wouldn't be able to sleep tonight if you thought otherwise. All I could think about when we were fighting that thing was that I wouldn't be able to stand it if you got hurt because I couldn't protect you." His hand remained on top of mine, and I looked up into his eyes—so soft and deep and caring. Being with Blake felt *right*.

But an image of Danielle popped into my mind, and I yanked my hand out of his. He might be planning on breaking up with her, but right now, they were still together. And despite almost letting him kiss me on the playground, I didn't want to be an accessory to cheating. "I should go," I said, the words getting stuck in my throat.

"Right." He nodded. "Goodnight, Nicole. Sleep well."

I said bye, got out of the car, and walked to my house. He didn't drive away until I stepped inside.

Once in my room I collapsed onto my bed, so exhausted that it only took seconds to fall asleep.

CHAPTER TWENTY-TWO

My cell phone rang, jolting me awake. Kate's name flashed on the caller ID. Wiping sleep out of my eyes, I pushed the answer button and lifted the phone to my ear.

"I'm outside your house," she told me before I could say hi.

I rolled over and stared at the ceiling. "Already?" I mumbled, trying not to sound as tired as I felt.

"Did I wake you up?" She gasped. "We're supposed to be at the diner in 15 minutes!"

"I can get ready fast," I said. "I'll be there in a few."

She said bye, and I managed to pull myself out of bed and trudge over to my closet. What was right to wear for a day of Journeying towards the Shadows—

whatever that meant—and possibly fighting more monsters like the one from last night?

It would probably be best to go with something comfortable. So I threw on jeans, a long-sleeved t-shirt, a sweatshirt, and sneakers. The pink Nike swoosh reminded me of what Darius had told us in homeroom a few days ago about how the symbol is based on the Greek goddess of victory.

It wasn't exactly battle armor, but it would have to do.

I walked downstairs and found my mom busy in the kitchen, cleaning up from dinner last night. She started the dishwasher and turned to me. "You slept late today," she said, pushing her hair out of her face. "Is everything all right?"

"I had trouble falling asleep," I told her. "But I'm heading out to have brunch with some friends—Kate's here to pick me up. They're giving me a tour of town afterwards, so I'll be out for a bit."

It wasn't *exactly* a lie.

"You've mentioned Kate before," she said, taking a glass out of the cabinet and filling it with water. "But who else are you going with?"

"Three other kids in my homeroom." I glanced at my watch to see how much time had passed. Five minutes. Hopefully Kate wouldn't be too mad. "Chris, Blake, and Danielle."

"Two guys," she said, waggling her eyebrows. "Are either of them cute?"

"Moooom," I whined, not in the mood to deal with this right now.

"Never mind," she said with a smile. "I'm just glad you're making friends so quickly. Call me when you know what time you'll be getting home. We should do something as a family tonight—maybe go out to dinner."

"Okay," I said, even though there was a chance that I might not be home in time for dinner.

My phone dinged—a text from Kate telling me to get outside—and I grabbed my coat and headed out the door.

CHAPTER TWENTY-THREE

"Took you long enough," Kate said as I got into the car.

"Sorry," I apologized again. "I had to get ready and let my mom know where I was going."

"It's okay," she said. "I just hate being late." She turned up the radio and sped down my street.

She was focused on driving, so I looked out the window as we made our way through town. It didn't take long to arrive at the diner. It looked different in the day—the neon sign wasn't lit, so the building looked more washed up, but it was just as busy inside. Waiters scurried around to get customers their food, although because it was morning most people had fluffy pancakes or Belgian waffles instead of hamburgers. It smelled delicious.

Chris waved at us from the same table we had yesterday. "You made it!" he said, scooting over to make room.

Kate rushed to sit next to Chris, which left me across from Blake. He was studying the menu as if he hadn't been there a million times before, refusing to make eye contact with me. I curled my fists under the table, trying to push away how much it hurt that he was blatantly ignoring me again.

Kate ran her hands through her hair and looked at Chris. "Nicole had trouble waking up." She laughed. "But it's okay. I dragged her out of bed."

"I couldn't fall asleep last night." I opened my straw and put it in my water—anything to avoid accidentally meeting Blake's eyes.

The waitress took our orders, and I got the full eggs, pancakes, and bacon meal. The fact that I had such a huge appetite surprised me. I should have been nervous about whatever was going to happen on our journey, but my stomach felt hollow, like I hadn't eaten in days. Maybe it was because of all the energy I'd expended recently.

After the waitress left, Chris slid into a casual conversation about school and sports. Kate smiled and nodded, clearly trying to appear not as worried as she was about all of the prophecy stuff. Danielle sent a few hate-glares in my direction, and Blake still wouldn't look at me. At least Chris had a talent for holding up a conversation on his own—especially when it involved talking about how he planned on using his power over air to increase his accuracy at shooting three-pointers.

I waited for Blake to bring up the incident from last night, but the food arrived before he had a chance. I contemplated bringing it up myself, but I couldn't do that. Because telling everyone about the two-headed hound also meant telling them that Blake and I had gone out together last night. There was no way to say it without angering Danielle. And the last thing we needed right now was extra drama.

I studied my food as I ate, my thoughts wandering. Even if Blake broke up with Danielle, the five of us were connected because of this prophecy. And as much as I wasn't a fan of Danielle's, starting something with Blake so soon after they broke up would be cruel. I would hate it if someone did something like that to me.

"So, are you all ready to get started?" Chris asked after we'd finished eating.

My thoughts drifted back to the monstrous hound. The anger in its glowing eyes was unlike anything I'd ever seen, and the way its two heads came out of the same body wasn't natural. If we had to face anything similar today, we weren't ready to handle it. At least I wasn't.

"You look worried," Kate said to me. "Is everything all right?"

"Yeah." I forced a smile. "I was just thinking about stuff."

She frowned. "If you want to wait until another day when you're more ready for this ..."

"No," I interrupted, placing my hands on the table.

"We have to do this today."

Danielle laughed, downed the last drops of her coffee, and placed the mug on the table. "Is this another one of your 'feelings?'" she asked.

Blake glared at her, and then turned his attention to me. His eyes were full of apology, but he said nothing. His silence hurt more than anything he could have said.

I zeroed in on Danielle, trying to remain calm and ignore her haughty expression. "We agreed to start now, so that's what we're going to do," I said, glad when Kate and Chris nodded in agreement.

Blake looked at his watch. "You said you wanted to do this when the sun was out, so now's the perfect time," he said. "It's almost noon, when the sun will be at its highest place in the sky."

Renewed energy hummed through my body, and I wondered if it was because the sun was shining, or because I'd just had a full meal. Probably a little bit of both.

Whatever it was, I was ready to hit the road and decipher that prophecy.

CHAPTER TWENTY-FOUR

Kate wanted to drive, and Chris jumped in front, leaving Blake, Danielle, and I to figure out the seating arrangements in back. Danielle immediately volunteered for the middle. At first I was disappointed that I wouldn't sit next to Blake, but it was for the best. I didn't want to deal with the awkwardness of my leg accidentally brushing his for the entire ride.

I looked out the window so I wouldn't have to see Danielle and Blake in my peripheral vision, watching the scenery as we drove down Odessa Road. We passed the news station where my dad worked, and then the road split. Kate veered left to stay on Odessa, driving past the entrance to the Hemlock Center. It looked a lot less foreboding during the day. Across from the Hemlock Center was an old cemetery. The rows of graves appeared to go on for miles.

As we got closer to the shore, the houses grew larger. Lots of them had boats parked outside. Finally we hit the small parking lot that looked out towards the ocean cove. No other cars were there. Branches scattered along the beach made it look like no one had walked there since summer.

Danielle crossed her legs, banging her foot against my shin. "This got us far," she said, rolling her eyes and looking out my window. "So much for your theory of driving east. If we drive any further, we'll end up in the ocean."

I looked out the window again and placed my hand against it. The waves crashed steadily on top of each other, creating foams of white water that lapped up onto the shore. "I don't know if the theory was wrong," I said. "We might as well explore."

"Why do you say that?" Danielle asked.

"I just have a feeling," I said. "Come on." I took my seatbelt off, climbed out of the car, and walked to the edge of the parking lot. I didn't care if they followed or not—I wanted to check it out for myself.

Shaped like a U, the beach wound its way around the cove. There were two docks sticking out into the water, both with boats tethered to the sides. The taste of salt filled the air, and small hills lined the perimeter. The rocky beach was so unlike the smooth sand I remembered from vacations to the Georgia shore when I was younger. Another gust of wind blew through the air, and the waves crashed down harder on top of one another, like the ocean was urging me closer.

The car doors slammed behind me, and I turned around to find the others walking in my direction. Kate and Chris led the way, Blake and Danielle trudging behind them. The only one who looked happy was Chris.

"Where do we go from here?" he asked, holding his hand above his eyes to block out the sun. "I can hotwire one of those boats if you need me to."

"*You* can hotwire?" Blake snickered. "I'd love to see that."

"We're not stealing any boats, so hotwiring won't be necessary," I said, even though the image of Chris trying to do that was amusing. "But I feel like we're in the right place. I just don't know what we're supposed to do now that we're here." I looked up at the sun, hoping an idea would come to me. Obviously our Greek deity ancestors weren't going to float down from Olympus and talk to us, but didn't they have other divine ways of intervening?

"That dock," Danielle said, pointing towards the one on the left.

Had she lost her mind? The dilapidated, crooked dock was clearly the older of the two. It looked like it might collapse into the water the second anyone walked on it. Only two boats with faded paint that probably hadn't been used for years were secured to the sides, as opposed to the clusters of modern, shinier boats bound to the newer dock on the right.

"Maybe we should try the other one," Kate said. "It looks safer..."

"No." Danielle shook her head. "It's that one." She marched to the decaying dock, the stilettos of her knee-high boots sinking into the sand with every step she took.

I followed her, my shoes spraying sand behind me as I hurried to catch up. The others followed as well. The uneven, jagged dock appeared just as unsteady up close as it did from far away. It creaked every time a wave hit. But that didn't stop Danielle—she walked down the dock like a model strutting the runway.

"It's down there," she said, pointing at the water next to the dock.

"*What's* down there?" I asked.

"Whatever we're here to get."

Kate wrapped her arms around herself and glanced back at the beach. "We should go back," she said. "We can look at the prophecy again and see if we missed something."

"Go back?" Chris's eyes widened. "Let's at least see what Danielle means. We've gone on instincts until now, and so far we've been right. Who's to say that she doesn't know what she's talking about?"

"Exactly," Danielle said. "I'm checking this out. You guys can stay or go, but there's something there, and I'm going to find out what it is."

"How do you know there's something there?" Blake asked softly, placing a hand on her elbow.

"It's…" Danielle paused, glancing at the water again and pressing her lips together. "Calling to me." She looked down at her nails, and I couldn't blame her for being embarrassed—it sounded crazy.

My fingertips were turning numb from the cold, and I pulled the sleeves of my coat over my hands. "Do you have any idea what 'it' is?" I asked her.

"Something important." She held her gaze with mine, not backing down.

"Okay," I said. "And how do you plan on getting it?"

"I'll jump."

I did a double take of her outfit—designer jeans, a blue silk shirt, a black winter coat with fur lining the hood, and, of course, the knee-high stiletto boots. It wasn't exactly the correct attire for jumping into the ocean in the winter.

"You'll freeze to death," Blake said what was surely on all of our minds. "And you're not dressed for swimming."

"I'll be fine." She didn't even flinch at the fact that she would ruin what was probably more than a thousand dollars worth of clothing. "Water is sort of my thing."

I said nothing, because if any of us were going to jump into the ocean in the middle of January, it would be Danielle.

Chris let out an uneasy laugh. "What are you going to do—change the temperature of the ocean to turn it into a giant hot tub? Because the ocean is kind of ... big."

"Thanks, Genius." Danielle rolled her eyes. "I realized that."

"Just trying to help." He grinned and flipped his hair out of his eyes.

"You should try," I threw my opinion out there. If

Danielle's instincts were correct, she could be helping us on the journey referred to in the prophecy.

She could also become hypothermic and drown, but I suspected that wouldn't be the case.

"I wasn't asking for your permission, even if you *are* in the center of all this," she said to me. Her tone was as cold as the weather, and everyone went quiet. The only sounds were the whooshing of the wind and the crashing waves. "I'm doing this, and don't any of you try to stop me."

She spun on her heel and dove off the dock, icy water splashing up at us as she disappeared beneath the surface.

CHAPTER TWENTY-FIVE

I stared at the place where Danielle had disappeared, waiting for her to resurface. But the water remained calm. There was no trace of her—she'd dove so deep that she was impossible to see.

"I'm going in after her." Blake widened his stance and studied the water, like he was building the courage to jump.

"No. You can't do that," I said, taking a step towards him. He stared at me, shocked—and a little annoyed—that I'd told him what to do. But I hated the thought of Blake getting hurt, so I continued, "Danielle has power over the water. You don't. She'll be fine, but you'll freeze to death if you go in there."

Chris stepped closer to the edge of the dock. "So

we're supposed to do nothing?" he asked. "She could be drowning, and you want us to stand here and watch?"

"Yes." Kate nodded. "She's the one who has power over water, and she seemed confident that she could handle this. She's most likely fine, but if any of us go in there, the water will be so cold that we won't be able to tell which way is up. Let's give Danielle a chance. She's *supposed* to do this. If she wasn't, she wouldn't be the only one who could 'hear' whatever she was talking about."

"Or maybe she's losing her mind," Chris said, looking worriedly at the spot where she'd jumped. "No one can stay under water for this long."

"Chris is right," Blake said through gritted teeth, the tension in his jaw visible as he spoke. "We have to help her. I'm going in after her." He took off his shoes and threw his coat to the ground, diving into the ocean before any of us could say no.

I stared at the spot where he'd disappeared. A sinking feeling passed through my stomach, growing worse when he didn't resurface. Now was the time to create a brilliant plan to save them both, but I froze, unable to think of anything. Too much time was passing. Danielle might be able to stay under for this long, but Blake couldn't.

He could be dying, and I was powerless to help him.

"Should we still do nothing?" Chris asked, his voice shaking. "Since it's working so well."

The water stirred, and Danielle's head popped out of the surface, her hair matted in place, mascara dripping down her cheeks. There was an arm wrapped around her shoulders—Blake's. He floated next to her, unconscious. She treaded water, the muscles in her face strained from holding onto him, but she managed to keep his head above the surface.

"Which one of you idiots let him jump in after me?" she yelled.

I met her death glare with one of my own. "None of us *let* him," I said, my throat tightening at the sight of Blake floating next to her. "He jumped before we could stop him."

She reached the dock and eased his arm from her shoulders, and Chris hurried to the edge to lift him up. Blake's body thumped as it hit the wood. His eyes were closed, his lips a sickly shade of blue, and his face was so chalky that he looked like a mix between an ancient statue and a corpse.

If he was dead ... I wasn't sure if my healing powers extended that far. Just the thought made chest hollow, and I clenched my fists so tightly that my nails dug into my palms. He *had* to be okay.

I ran over to him and held my hand to his cheek, unaware of the tears streaming down my face until they landed on his pale skin. Then I felt a faint glow of life coming from his body. He was alive. So there had to be something I could do.

This was nothing like fixing a cut, but I grabbed his hand anyway, determined to heal him.

Instead of closing my eyes, I kept them open, focusing on his pale face as I pulled white energy out of the air. Warmth rushed through my veins, energy pulsing through my body as the center of our palms opened to each other, and I pushed the energy I'd gathered towards him. Just when it felt like I wouldn't be able to pull out any more energy from the Universe, his eyes snapped open, and he leaned to the side to cough the water out of his lungs.

My head felt fuzzy, like I was about to pass out myself, but that didn't matter right now. All that mattered was that Blake was okay.

Danielle rushed over to him and wrapped her arms around him, shoving me to the side. My elbow collided with the dock, a sharp pain shooting up my arm. I rubbed it, glaring at her. I'd just saved Blake's life. She could at least pretend to be grateful.

"What happened?" he asked, his voice hoarse.

"You jumped into the ocean to try saving me and nearly drowned," she said, laughing and crying at the same time. "As if I needed saving. Water's my element."

I sat up and healed my elbow, stopping the throbbing that would surely turn into a bruise in the next few hours. Then I looked over at Danielle. She had been dripping wet a second ago, but now she—and her clothes—were completely dry.

She was more powerful than I'd realized.

She took Blake's hand—the same hand I'd held while saving his life—and all of the water soaking his clothes glided off him, forming a puddle on the dock and slithering back to the ocean.

"Thanks," he said, running his hands through his now-dry hair.

"Of course." She reached for his hand, and while he didn't grab it back, he didn't drop it, either. He just let it sit in his.

"Did you find what you were looking for?" he asked her.

"I almost got it before you jumped in after me," she said, laughing now that it was clear he was going to be fine. "Now I have to go back in and get it."

It was tempting to say something about how at least he'd cared enough to *try* helping her, but I kept my mouth shut.

Kate frowned and looked at Danielle. "What exactly *was* it that you were looking for?" she asked.

"Some sort of jar," Danielle replied. "It looked tied down, or attached to a stone, but I'm going to try getting it anyway."

"It can't hurt to try," Chris agreed. Then he looked at Blake and said, "And don't go playing Superman again. Or I guess Aquaman would make more sense."

"Don't worry." Blake smirked. "I'll leave that to Danielle. I've had enough of swimming in the freezing cold ocean for the day."

"All right," Danielle said. "Here goes nothing." She spun on her heel and dove back in, not creating a splash this time. It was like she'd become part of the water.

Figuring it would be at least a minute until she returned, I checked to see how Blake was doing. His face and lips had returned to a healthy color. Another rush of relief passed through my body, and I realized that if he hadn't helped me practice using my powers last night, he could be dead right now. My throat tightened at the thought, and I swallowed to make the lump go away.

"I'm glad you're okay," I said, stepping towards him.

"Thanks to you," he said. "I don't know what you did, but..." He paused, his eyes full of concern. "It didn't drain too much of your energy, right?"

"I'll be fine," I said, although I suspected that if I had to do whatever I'd done for a bit longer, it might have become a problem. "I'll just take it easy for the next hour or so."

The probability of that happening was slim-to-none, but no one said anything otherwise.

"Just don't go fighting any monsters," he said with a wink.

I stood still, not knowing how to respond. Kate and Chris still didn't know about the two-headed hound from last night. That must have sounded completely strange to them.

Kate shuffled her feet and looked back and forth between the two of us. "Right," she said, her forehead scrunched. "No monster fighting. I'll keep that in mind."

Danielle resurfaced before I could respond, and she lifted a large object into the air. "I got it!" she exclaimed.

I squinted, trying to make out what she was holding. It looked like a jar with two handles. The deep orange background reminded me of red clay before it's put into the kiln, and brown images decorated the sides. I was too far away to make out what they were.

She swam to the dock and placed the jar down. Then she hoisted herself up, the wooden planks creaking under her weight. She was already completely dry. The jar was dry as well.

Kate knelt in front of the jar and reached forward to touch it, but she pulled her hand back at the last second, as if afraid of damaging it. "This is beautiful," she said. "Look at the details in the paintings."

I knelt down next her to get a better look. While the paintings on the jar were tiny, they held more detail than I ever could have imagined. The largest section featured a bearded man in an elegant chariot pulled by a horse, his hair blowing in the wind, a surge of water coming up behind him. His eyes looked fiercely outward, and he held a trident in his hand. Packs of horses galloped around the chariot, and a winged horse in the sky looked down on him. He had to be Poseidon—the god of the sea.

"It's like Pandora's Jar," Kate whispered, still fixated on the paintings.

"Jar?" I sat back on my heels and looked at her. "I thought Pandora had a box."

"There was a mistranslation from Greek to Latin," she explained. "It was actually a jar."

"And this is the jar from the myth?" I tilted my head in disbelief. That sounded pretty far-fetched.

"No." She shook her head. "Not the same jar. Although Pandora's Jar was created by Hephaestus— the god of fire, blacksmiths, and artisans. Maybe he created this one, too."

"Maybe," I said, although I doubted it. Greek gods

didn't just come down to Earth and drop handmade jars into the ocean. Actually, from what Darius said in class the other day, the gods rarely came down to Earth at all.

Danielle scooted closer and held her hands above the jar. "I'm going to open it," she announced, looking at each of us for confirmation. No one said anything—we all knew she was going to open it whether we agreed or not—and she wrapped her fingers around the handle, easing it upward like she was afraid it might break.

I braced myself for something crazy to happen—an explosion, a flash of light, a sonic boom. But the jar remained the same.

Danielle leaned forward to see what was inside, her hair draping in front of her face. "There's a piece of paper in there," she said, lowering her hand into the jar. Something shuffled inside, and she brought out a piece of rolled up parchment. It reminded me of the one Darius had showed me of the original prophecy. However, unlike the prophecy, which was yellowed with curled edges, this parchment was as good as new. It was also completely dry.

"It's immune to the elements." Kate's mouth formed into a small circle. She leaned forward, tucking her hair behind her ears as she examined the paper. "The jar had to have been crafted by Hephaestus. Almost every magical, finely-made object is."

Danielle unrolled the paper and examined it.

"What does it say?" Kate asked.

"Travel north to the King of the Sky," she began, her

voice rising as she continued, "He stands amongst the stones of the dead, accessible to the one who can fly high." She lowered the parchment and looked at each of us, like she was waiting for one us to tell her what it meant.

"Fly north to the sky?" Chris looked up at the sun and used his hand as a visor, squinting in the direct light. "Anyone got a private plane? Or a rocket?"

Kate laughed, but she sounded more on edge than anything else. "I don't think that's what it means, especially considering that when this was written three hundred years ago, people had no way to get up there."

"But it's a *prophecy*." Chris elongated the last word. "Sure, they didn't have planes yet, but they could prophesize their existence."

Danielle played with the paper, looking back and forth between Chris and Kate. "The prophecy got us what we needed by driving east, so now we should head north," she said, glancing back at the car in the parking lot.

Thinking back over the ride to the ocean, an idea popped into my mind. "The stones of the dead," I repeated, surprised I hadn't realized it immediately. "The cemetery. We passed it on the way here."

"Of course." Kate snapped her fingers. "The statue of Zeus—the King of the Sky."

"There's a statue of Zeus in the cemetery?" I asked. That was the most random thing I'd heard all day.

"Right in the back of it," Blake said. "It's taller than a house. We always figured our ancestors put it there to remind us where we came from. Urban legend says it's haunted, so middle schoolers like to sneak out to the cemetery at night to see if anything happens."

"And does it?" I asked.

"No." He laughed. "That's why it's called an urban legend."

"Right," I said. Urban legends: fiction. Greek mythology: fact. I would have to remember that. "Then what's so important about the statue?"

"You've heard of the Seven Wonders of the World, right?" Kate asked, standing up and stretching her arms behind her back.

"Like the Great Wall of China and the Taj Mahal?"

"Those are the Seven Wonders of the *Medieval* World," she explained. "Same idea, but it's based off the Seven Wonders of the Ancient World."

"So ..." I paused to recall the old monuments I'd learned about in school. "The Pyramid of Giza?"

Kate nodded, a small smile forming on her lips. "That's the only one still in existence today," she said. "One of the other Ancient Wonders is the Statue of Zeus at Olympia. There's a replica right here in the Kinsley cemetery. Art History professors come here all the time to check it out, but the Parthenon in Nashville attracts more tourists because it's way more famous."

"There's a Parthenon in Nashville?" I asked.

She nodded again. "Because of all the higher education institutions there, Nashville's called 'the Athens of the South,'" she said, making quote signs with her hands. "The city built it in the late 1800's.

But the Statue of Zeus here is where the idea of recreating ruined monuments in the States came from. It was built ten years before Nashville's Parthenon."

Danielle clanked the lid back on the jar and picked it up. "Enough with the history lesson," she said, hugging the jar to her chest. "The statue is super close, and it's the best thing we have to go on. So let's check it out."

CHAPTER TWENTY-SIX

Zeus towered over the mausoleums, rivaling the height of the nearby birch trees. He sat on top of a podium that was about seven feet tall. Carved mythological scenes decorated the sides of his throne, and his left hand held a scepter with an eagle on top. His right hand balanced what looked like an angel in his palm. His shoulder length hair and long beard resembled the image of Poseidon on the jar, but while the Sea God's hair blew loosely in the wind, Zeus's was symmetrical, not a strand out of place. His eyes stared forward—powerful and determined.

"That's incredible," I said, my lips parted in awe.

Even though Kate must have seen the statue before, her eyes were wide as she took it in. "It really is," she said. "It's an exact reproduction of the original. It's made of ivory, the throne is wood with gold painted carvings, and Zeus's hair, beard, and clothing are all made of gold. I never get bored of looking at it."

I didn't bother to ask how she knew all of that. Knowing Kate, she'd researched it eons ago and still remembered every detail.

"You see the goddess that Zeus is holding?" she asked, pointing to the figure in his right hand.

The goddess was what I'd originally thought was an angel. Tiny compared to Zeus, she stood proudly in his palm, her wings wide open behind her. She held one hand up in the air, pointing forward like she was preparing for battle.

I nodded for Kate to continue.

"That's the goddess Nike," she explained. "The goddess of victory that Darius told you about during your first day of class. Now do you see how her wings look like the swoosh?"

I walked around to look at the goddess from the side. "Sort of," I said. "But I wouldn't have noticed unless someone had pointed it out."

"You guys can study the statue all you want another day," Danielle said. "But we're looking for something here, and we should try to figure out what it is. Maybe it's another jar."

"What did the clue say again?" Chris asked, scanning the statue up and down.

Danielle didn't unroll the paper, instead reciting the

clue from memory. "Travel north to the King of the Sky. He stands amongst the stones of the dead, accessible to the one who can fly high."

"It's not a jar this time," Chris said. "It's the eagle. The one at the top of Zeus's scepter."

"How do you know that?" Kate asked.

"Danielle said the jar was calling to her." He looked at Danielle, and she nodded in affirmation. "Well, the eagle is glowing, like it has an aura. It's faint, but it's definitely there."

I craned my neck up to look at the eagle at the top of Zeus's scepter. It wasn't glowing. But then again, I hadn't "heard" when the jar called to Danielle either.

Kate studied the statue, her lips pursed. "How do you propose we get up there?" she said.

Chris smiled mischievously and wiggled his eyebrows. "Are you up for some fun?" he asked her.

"It depends on how you define 'fun,'" she said. "Because if you're implying that we climb the statue, then I'm going to have to say no. I want to get through this day alive, and falling to my death from sixty feet in the air doesn't seem like an effective way to do that."

"I wasn't implying that we *climb*." He laughed and flipped his hair out of his eyes. "I'll swirl you up in the air like I did with the paper yesterday and you can grab the eagle. It'll be easy." He flicked his fingers around in a circle, blowing some leaves off the ground to demonstrate.

"Swirl me in the air?" Kate's mouth dropped open. "I would rather climb."

"Come on," he pleaded. "We need to get up there

somehow. And it'll be fun."

She crossed her arms and shook her head. "Why are you asking me?" she said. "Can't someone else do it?"

"I'll do it," I offered, cursing myself a second later for volunteering. I hated heights.

"No," Blake cut in. "You need to rest after using all that energy at the ocean. We need you at full strength in case you need to heal someone again, and you won't be able to do that if you're dead." He paused, his eyes softening as if he realized how harsh that sounded. "If you even *can* die, which isn't something we should experiment with right now. Or ever."

"Right." I turned away from him to look back at Chris, glad that I wouldn't have to fly up there. "I guess that leaves Blake, Kate or Danielle."

"Fine." Kate huffed and held up a hand. "I'll do it. I weigh the least, so it makes sense."

"Awesome!" Chris beamed, rubbing his hands together. "You ready?"

"As I'll ever be." She sounded less than enthused. "When I get up there, I'm just supposed to grab the eagle? What if it doesn't come off?"

"The jar was practically part of a rock," Danielle jumped in. "But I could pull it right out."

"Yeah." Chris pointed his thumb in Danielle's direction. "What she said."

"Great." Kate forced a smile and looked up at the towering statue. "I can do this. I'm ready." It sounded like she was trying to convince herself more than us.

"All right." Chris pointed to the ground near Zeus.

"Stand there."

Kate looked at me with bulging eyes, and I smiled in encouragement before she headed over to the spot. If Chris dropped her, at least I would be able to heal her. Well, if the fall didn't kill her on impact. I didn't know if my power extended to bringing people back from the dead. If it did ... I shivered at the thought. That wasn't something I wanted to have to find out.

"Here it goes!" Chris narrowed his eyes in concentration as he looked at Kate. He lifted his hand and held it out toward her, his palm facing forward. But he didn't create a mini-tornado like with the paper at Blake's house yesterday. Instead the air pushed against the bottoms of Kate's feet, lifting her up like a hot air balloon. She gave little kicks with her legs as she rose.

"That's good," she said, her voice shaky. "Not too fast."

I half-expected Chris to shoot her ten feet in the air just to be snarky, but he listened, letting her float upward until she arrived at the top of the statue. She reached forward and secured her arms around the eagle. It looked about the same size as the jar Danielle had brought up from the ocean, but standing sixty feet below, I couldn't be sure.

Kate gave it a tug, but it stayed in place. "It's too heavy!" she screamed. "There's no way I can lift it."

"Try harder!" Chris yelled back up at her. "The eagle's what we need. I know it."

She lost her grip after the third yank, her arms flailing back to her sides. "It won't work." She looked down at us and shrugged. "This is impossible."

Chris scrunched his eyebrows. "Are you sure?"

Kate gave the eagle another unsuccessful tug. "Yes." She placed her hands on her hips, which looked funny while she was floating in the air. "Can you please let me down now?"

"Fine." He lowered his hands, his brows furrowed as he controlled the air holding Kate up. She floated to the ground and landed as lightly as a feather.

She jogged towards us, pushing her hair behind her ears. "Sorry," she apologized to Chris. "I tried. I just wasn't strong enough. That thing wasn't budging."

"I don't understand what went wrong," he said, studying the eagle perched on the top of Zeus's scepter. "I *know* that's the key to whatever comes next."

"You should try getting it," Danielle suggested, pointing at Chris. "Maybe it's not working for Kate because it's *your* clue to uncover. My jar came out just fine."

"You mean the object only comes loose for the person it's meant for?" Chris scratched his head. "Like there's some sort of spell on it?"

"It's just an idea," she said. "You should try to fly yourself up there. Worst comes to worst, it doesn't work."

"Or I fall and crack my head open," he muttered.

Kate jerked her head to look at him, her mouth open in a circle of disbelief. "You lifted me up there with no problem," she said. "Why do you think you can't do the same for yourself?"

"It just seems impossible." He glanced at the statue again, doubt crossing over his eyes. "But I'll try."

Kate's lips curved into a small smile. "Good."

"If you fall, you always have Nicole to fix you up," Danielle said with a snicker.

"Exactly." I ignored Danielle's attitude and smiled at Chris. "You'll be fine. You're stronger than you think. And I can heal you if you need it."

"All right." He walked to the statue to stand below the scepter, took a deep breath, and closed his eyes. "It's not working!" he said. But then he opened his fists so his palms pointed towards his feet, and he started to rise—faster than Kate had when he'd lifted her. The wind blew his hair in all directions. When he reached the halfway point, he soared upward until he was level with the eagle. "Look at that!" he shouted, lifting his arms in the air and pointing his toes towards the ground. "I'm Superman!"

He *did* look like he was flying, except it was more like he was standing on a puff of air, his legs wobbling as he tried to stay balanced. He wrapped his hands around the eagle just like Kate had and lifted it off the scepter. He didn't have to strain at all.

He laughed and looked down at Kate. "You had trouble doing *that*?" he said, raising the eagle over his head like a trophy. "I must be stronger than I thought!"

"Or Danielle was right and the eagle would only come off for you," Kate muttered, rolling her eyes. I couldn't help but laugh.

Chris floated down to the ground and ran toward

us. "I got it!" he said again, his arms wrapped around the eagle.

"What do we do with it now?" I asked.

He lowered it to the ground, the muscles in his arms tightening as he placed it down. The eagle was the same height as the jar—it nearly reached my knee—its wings spread out like it was about to take flight. Each feather was meticulously carved to the point where they could have been real, and its eyes were hard and determined, like Zeus's.

Chris kneeled down to study it, craning his head to look at it from different angles. "There's a line right here," he said, pointing to a thin crack that formed a complete circle around the eagle's neck. "Maybe its head is a lid, like Danielle's jar."

He reached forward to lift it off, but Danielle shoved her hand in front of his, stopping him. "Let Kate try," she said, her eyes hard as she looked at Chris.

He kept his hand poised above the eagle. "Why?" he asked.

"Because then we'll see if only *you* can open it, just like only *you* could lift it off the statue." She annunciated each word, like Chris was too stupid to understand. "If Kate can't get it open—or any of us, for that matter—then we know that the only person who can open each object is whoever is 'supposed' to."

While I didn't want to say it out loud, Danielle did have a good point.

The four of us took turns attempting to get the head off the eagle, each with no success. I saw the line that looked like a lid, but it might as well have been welded shut. That thing was *not* budging.

"Now it's your turn." Danielle motioned for Chris to try.

He rubbed his hands together. "I've got the magic touch," he said, kneeling down and wrapping his fingers around the eagle's head. It popped right off. He reached inside and pulled out a rolled piece of parchment the same size as the one Danielle had found in her jar.

"What does it say?" I asked, resisting the urge to grab it out of his hands so I could read it myself.

He unrolled the paper and held it in front of him. "Follow the direction of Victory, as she will lead to the fuel that burns the fire. That which causes destruction can also be used for creation." He shrugged and looked back up. "That's all I've got. And Victory is capitalized."

"The direction of Victory..." I said, looking up at the goddess in Zeus's hand. "It could mean Nike. Didn't Sophie say that Nike meant victory?"

Danielle stood up and wiped some dirt off her jeans. "It's just another vague clue," she muttered. "This would be easier if they could give us a map."

"The fuel that burns the fire," Blake repeated, looking at Nike. "She's pointing to the woods."

I faced the direction of Nike's finger. "That's northwest," I said.

I had no idea how I knew that—but I knew I was right.

"Those are the woods near Darius's house, right?" Kate asked. "The ones we stood next to on the night of the comet."

"Clenton Woods," Chris said, rolling the paper back up. "I live a few houses down from Darius. I used to play in those woods when I was younger." He placed the paper back in the eagle and shut the lid. "Let's go check this out."

CHAPTER TWENTY-SEVEN

We drove on Odessa Road until reaching the woods. Once there, Kate parked in Chris's driveway. The trees here were taller than the ones in Georgia, and they had more branches. In the winter they looked like skeletons, but I imagined they must be pretty in the summer with all of their leaves.

"Where to now?" Danielle asked Blake. "Do you hear something calling to you?"

"Or see something glowing?" Chris added.

"No..." Blake said, looking out into the woods. "Why don't we walk around and see what we can find?"

"There are a few trails around here." Chris walked towards the woods and motioned for us to follow. "They shouldn't be too far. Some friends and I used to go to this abandoned cottage to play around in before my parents found out what we were doing. It had burned down a long time ago, and they said it wasn't safe. They were afraid we would get hurt."

"A cottage that burned down?" I repeated, surprised he hadn't mentioned it earlier. "We should check it out. It works with the whole fire-destruction thing in the clue."

"The trail should be right around … here." Chris stopped at a small break in the trees.

It looked like an animal path—barely wide enough for an average-sized person. I probably wouldn't have noticed it unless Chris had pointed it out. There was just enough room to walk if you ducked under the occasional branch and watched out for tree roots.

I glanced at Danielle to see her reaction to hiking in her stilettos. She had a look of disgust plastered on her face, which amused me. She would jump into a freezing cold ocean, but was horrified at the idea of walking through the woods. I didn't think I would ever understand her.

Kate glided past us, pushing through a group of branches and walking underneath them. "Come on," she teased. "The trees aren't going to hurt you."

Chris and Blake followed her, leaving Danielle and me standing at the opening. "After you," I said, motioning for her to go ahead. She jogged to catch up with the others, stumbling over a tree root in the process. I followed as close behind as possible, managing to accumulate a fair share of scratches on my hands from the branches. I contemplated saving my energy and not healing the small cuts, but they stung, so I fixed them anyway. Using a tiny bit of energy wouldn't make too much of a difference. If anything, it was practice.

"Here it is," Chris said from up ahead. I followed Danielle, who was stumbling in her stilettos, and we caught up with the group.

We were standing in a small clearing, most of it taken up by the remnants of the deteriorating cottage. It looked like it only had two rooms before it had burned down. The charred wooden planks making up the floor had warped into themselves, and the log walls barely existed anymore. Mounds of stones made up what appeared to have been a fireplace. Nature was reclaiming most of the cottage—moss grew everywhere, and trees were sprouting up on the inside.

I could see why Chris's parents didn't want him playing there as a child. The place was just asking for someone to get hurt.

Blake looked at the house, his jaw tense. "Does it feel warmer here than in the rest of the woods?" he asked, studying the center of the warped floor.

A cold breeze passed through the air, the tree branches whistling in the wind. "I wish," I said, pulling the sleeves of my jacket over my hands.

He walked towards the cottage and stepped over what was left of the wall, his eyes intense as he focused on that same spot in the center of the floor.

"Are you sure that's safe to walk on?" Danielle asked.

Blake glanced at her over his shoulder and laughed.

"Says the girl who jumped in the ocean when it's below freezing outside."

"Fair point," she mumbled, taking a step back.

The wood creaked beneath Blake's feet, and he was careful not to step on any parts that looked like they were about to cave in. Once at the center, he knelt down and pressed his hand against a plank that looked relatively intact compared to the others surrounding it.

Kate looked at me and tilted her head. I shrugged, having no more of an idea what Blake was doing than anyone else.

"Want to tell us what's going on?" Danielle yelled, stepping forward and placing her hands on her hips. He didn't reply, so she jogged towards the ruined cottage and stepped over the edge. She took a few steps, but her stiletto got stuck between the boards and she tumbled to the ground, catching herself with the palms of her hands.

Apparently she wasn't as graceful on land as she was in the water.

She brushed the dirt off her palms and huffed, not making an effort to stand back up.

Blake looked over at her and smirked. "You know how you didn't need me to jump in the ocean after you?" he asked, continuing before she could respond. "Well, you don't have to help me here. I've got this covered."

He turned back around and took out his lighter, flicking it to life. He transferred the flames so they hovered in an orb over his hand. Just as he had on the playground, he controlled the fire perfectly, lowering it to the floorboards. The burning wood smelled like a campfire, crisp in the brisk winter air.

I wanted to get closer to warm my hands, but Blake had made it clear that he needed to do this on his own. Plus, the floor didn't look stable. I didn't want to fall like Danielle, who had rejoined us and was still brushing the dirt off her jeans.

Blake lifted one of the charred floorboards and removed something from under it. His back faced me, so I couldn't see what he'd found. Finally, he turned around, holding an iron box. It was smaller than the jar and the eagle—it looked about the size of a toolbox. He maneuvered his way out of the remnants of the cottage and dropped the box on the ground near our feet. Dirt poofed up from under it. The box must have been heavier than it looked.

"The clue must be inside." Kate reached for the lid, but it wouldn't open for her. "You try," she told Blake.

When Blake tried, the lid lifted without a fight. He reached inside and pulled out two items—a leather book, and another, smaller box that was also metal.

Danielle kneeled down next to the box. "Where's the clue?" she asked.

He opened the book, his eyebrows knitting together as he glanced through whatever was in it.

"Well?" she prompted.

"There's no clue here." He rubbed the back of his neck and paged through the book again. "All this has are instructions for how to make things."

I peered over his shoulder to see what he meant.

Diagrams were scattered all over the pages—instructions on how to create weapons. I shuddered at the thought. But then I thought about the monster from last night. If we had to face anything like that again, weapons would be useful to have around. I wouldn't always have metal monkey bars at my disposal.

Chris circled around Blake to get a look. "What kind of things?" he asked.

"Weapons." Blake lowered the book, his eyes hard. "It's full of instructions about how to forge weapons with fire."

"Cool." Chris frowned, not sounding as enthused as usual. "But why do we need weapons? We've got our powers." He swirled some leaves around for emphasis.

"I don't know." Blake closed the book and picked up the other, smaller box. He opened it and pulled something out that looked like an antique pocket watch. Five words were engraved on the top. They were written in Greek, but my mind automatically translated them: fire, water, air, and earth. In the center was the Greek word for spirit, or Aether.

Blake popped it open, revealing a black needle with a scripted gold K on the tip. Along the edges of the circle were four evenly dispersed gems—a ruby, emerald, topaz, and sapphire. A diamond sparkled in the center, the needle balanced on top of it.

"It looks like a compass," I said.

Danielle reached forward and grabbed it. "What does it mean by 'K?'" she asked.

"Was there an explanation in the book?" Kate asked

Blake.

"No," he said. "It's only instructions on how to forge weapons. But feel free to look for yourself."

Kate opened the book and paged through it. "You're right," she finally said. "There's no clue here. So I guess the obvious thing to do is follow the compass."

"Most compasses point north," I thought out loud. "But this one points northwest."

"How do you know that?" Danielle asked.

"I just do," I said. "Ever since moving here, I can 'feel' directions. But you're free to use the compass app on your phone to check for yourself."

She opened her app and calibrated the compass. "Fine ... you're right," she admitted. "The needle on the compass we found is pointing northwest, not north."

I was tempted to tell her that I told her so, but I held my tongue.

Blake looked back and forth between the two of us. "I guess we're going northwest," he said.

With that, he grabbed the box and led the way out of the woods.

CHAPTER TWENTY-EIGHT

Due to my newfound sense of direction, the group insisted that I sit in the passenger seat and navigate. Even Danielle agreed.

The compass continued to lead us northwest, so we kept driving up Odessa Road, so far that we passed Kinsley High. But after passing the school, something changed.

"It's moving," I told them, watching the arrow steadily rotate. "It's pointing east now."

"Towards the school?" Danielle leaned forward to see for herself. "All of this running around collecting clues and it's leading us to *school?*

"Not directly towards the school," I answered. "A little more south. It changed after the intersection of

Odessa Road and Beverly Street. There are woods just south of the school, right?"

Kate pulled into a side street and turned around. "Bosley Woods," she muttered. "Great."

"Is there something wrong with those woods?" I asked.

"No." She shook her head. "They just give me the creeps."

"Me, too," Chris piped up from the back. "They give off a weird vibe."

Creepy woods emitting weird vibes. Fantastic. It couldn't be worse than a cemetery, but Kate loved nature. If the woods made *her* jumpy, they had to be pretty bad.

Kate turned into the school. Only a few cars were parked in front, but other than that, the normally bustling lot was empty. "We can park near the gym," she said. "It's closest to the woods, and it should be empty since there isn't a game today."

She headed towards the gym, and for the first time since we'd gotten into the car, everyone was silent.

"It'll be fine, guys," Danielle tried to break the tension.

"Yeah," Chris said with more confidence. "We've already swam in freezing water, flown to the top of a sixty foot statue, and excavated a burned down cottage. We can handle whatever's coming next. We're the Elementals."

"The Elementals?" I laughed and glanced back at him.

"We needed a team name," he said sheepishly.

"Since we're going to be working together and all."

Danielle sat back in her seat. "It sounds like something from a comic book," she said. "We're witches—not superheroes."

"And you know this because ... you read comics?" I stifled laughter, since I couldn't picture that.

"No." She crossed her arms and stared out the window. It looked ridiculous, since she was squished in the middle seat between Chris and Blake.

Chris smiled and nudged her with his shoulder. "Don't lie," he teased. "You used to bring them to school and trade them with Matt in second grade."

"Matt?" I gasped. "You mean the human Chris introduced me to at the party last week? The one who's dating Anne?"

"That's right." Chris said, still smiling. "Before we were allowed to use our powers, there wasn't such a big difference between us and humans. Until ninth grade..." He paused, glancing at Danielle and Blake. "Or earlier for those of us who broke the rules. And if I remember right, Danielle didn't just trade comic books with Matt. Didn't the two of you have a thing?"

Blake smirked. "I remember that ..." he said. "Then your parents thought you were getting too close to a human and wouldn't let you go over his house to play anymore. You were devastated."

Danielle huffed and glared at Chris. "My parents knew what they were talking about," she said. "There was no reason for me to waste my time with a human. Besides, it was in second grade. We were seven. It doesn't count."

"Oh, it counts." Chris nodded his head dramatically. "Nicole," he continued, facing me. "What's your consensus on this?"

"Does this really matter?" Kate interrupted, parking and yanking the key out of the ignition. "Let's just check out the woods, follow the compass, and do whatever we're supposed to do."

We all climbed out of the car, and I studied the woods for the first time. Bosley Woods made Clenton Woods look like a welcoming palace. Just looking at them made me step backwards in revulsion. A gray mist hovered above the ground, ready to suck in anyone who walked on it, and the air smelled damp, like there was mold growing everywhere. The wind blew the tallest trees back and forth, and it sounded like the forest was groaning, warning people to keep out.

Still, the creepiness was more than what the forest *looked* like. Because staring at it made a bone-chilling cold wash through my body. My chest tightened the same way it had before the two-headed hound attacked Blake and me at the playground—like a warning to leave before it was too late.

I looked down at the compass in my hands. The needle pointed straight towards the woods. I shook it a few times to see if it would change its mind, but it stayed locked in place.

"This is the right place," I said, wishing I could tell them otherwise.

"Is it just me, or are the woods creepier than normal?" Chris asked, his teeth chattering.

Kate shivered and rubbed her arms. "They seem ... evil," she agreed. "If that makes any sense."

"It makes just as much sense as anything else that's happened recently." Danielle squinted like she was trying to see past the fog, which wove between the bottoms of the tree trunks like it had a life of its own.

Blake stared straight into the woods. If he was scared, I couldn't tell. "So are we doing this or what?" he asked.

The color drained from Chris's face, and he shifted his weight from one foot to the other. "Who's leading the way?" he asked.

Kate took a small step forward. "I guess I'll do it," she volunteered. "Earth is my element, which means this clue is mine. Whatever it is that we need to find next should be calling to me—or however it worked for the three of you." She turned to face me, standing straighter. "I'll need the compass," she said matter-of-factly. "Since it seems to be telling us where to go."

"Right." I held the compass out to her, and it felt good to get rid of it. Maybe Kate was supposed to have been controlling the compass all along, and because I'd been holding it, it hadn't pointed us in the right direction.

She took it from me, and the arrow stayed in place.

So much for that theory.

"Follow me." She took a deep breath, straightened her shoulders, and walked confidently towards the woods. I hoped the bravery wasn't just for show. With Earth being her element, Kate should be comfortable in places like this.

I walked through the opening to the woods, and a chill passed through my body. The forest held no traces of life. Grass had grown here at some point, but all of it was dead—browned and wilted, pressed to the ground like it had been trampled in a stampede.

I glanced over my shoulder to check on the others. Blake was only two feet behind me, having just stepped over the perimeter. He paused and met my gaze.

"Do you want me to go ahead of you?" he asked.

"I'm fine," I said, reminding myself that we were more powerful than any animal in these woods. We shouldn't have a problem protecting ourselves. "But thanks."

"No problem." He looked to where Kate waited next to a tree so big that it must have been hundreds of years old. "If anything tries to attack from behind, I've got your back. After all, I owe you."

I wondered if he was referring to when I saved him from hypothermia, helped him kill the monster last night, or both. But Kate was waiting for us, so I just said thanks, turned around, and jogged down the path to catch up with her.

"Scared?" Kate asked, a wry smile on her lips.

"A little." I looked up at the looming branches, arched like gnarled fingers about to reach down and snatch me up. "Like you said, the woods are creepy."

"They're just trees," she said. "They're not going to come alive and attack us. Plus, I get the feeling that it's not the trees that are evil. It's something else. Something hidden in the woods."

I wrapped my arms around myself and shivered. "With our luck, the compass is pointing right to that 'something,'" I said.

"We won't know until we get there."

With that, Kate turned around and led us towards wherever the compass was telling us to go next.

CHAPTER TWENTY-NINE

We trekked deeper into the woods, the tight feeling in my chest growing worse with every step. The further we got, the more the temperature dropped. The cold penetrated my bones, and I could barely feel my fingers or toes anymore.

"Are we almost there?" I asked Kate, stumbling on a twisted root. I caught myself and looked over my shoulder to see if anyone saw, my eyes instantly meeting Blake's. He smiled, and I turned around to continue walking, my cheeks heating from embarrassment.

"The path is getting wider," Kate called back. "Hopefully that's a good thing."

"Right," I muttered. The cold was growing worse

with each step, and I brought the ends of my sleeves together and held my hands inside of them, trying to get some feeling back into my fingers. I really needed to remember my gloves. I wished I were inside in front of a fire, sipping on hot chocolate like any normal person would be doing in the winter.

"I think this is it," Kate said from ahead.

I hurried to join her in a circular clearing. Just like the rest of the forest, the grass was dead and pressed to the ground. But the break in the trees allowed the sun to shine through, and I looked up, smiling as the warmth caressed my cheeks.

"What is this place?" Blake asked from beside me. He shivered and brought out his lighter, flicking it on to form a hovering ball of fire.

I took my hands out of my sleeves and held them over the light. My fingertips stung as the warmth returned to them. "Thanks," I said, pushing the pads of my fingers together to check if I could feel them. I could. "But you shouldn't use up too much energy. Whatever we have to do next ... well, I don't know what it will be, but I have a feeling that we're going to need to save up as much energy for it as we can."

Danielle joined us, also warming her hands up above the flame. "Nicole's right," she said. "You shouldn't use up too much energy."

Blake moved his hands to his sides, and the fire disappeared. The change of light made my vision spotty. I blinked a few times until it was back to normal and turned my focus back to Kate. She was staring down at the compass with wide eyes, her jaw dropped open.

"What is it?" I rushed to her side and looked at the compass, gasping at what I saw.

The needle spun around so quickly that it blended into the gold background, looking like it could break or fly right off at any second.

Kate snapped the compass shut, looked at each of us, and said, "I guess we've reached our destination."

CHAPTER THIRTY

"What now?" I asked, looking around the clearing again. It wasn't a circle like I'd originally thought—it was more of a semi-circle, curving around two huge trees.

"I'm going to ask the trees what we need to do," Kate resolved, marching over to the largest one.

"Did you just say 'ask the trees?'" Danielle laughed, her upper lip curled in disbelief.

Kate placed a hand on the side of the tree, not bothering to answer Danielle's question.

"Yep." Chris nodded, his lips pressed together. "She's 'asking the trees.' What *else* do you do when you're in the middle of a forest with a crazy compass and no clue what to do next?"

Kate held her hand against the trunk, her eyes closed. She stood like that for about half a minute. Then she lifted her hand off the tree.

The ground grumbled, so loud that it could have been Hades trying to escape from the underworld. Then the tree roots shifted. They moved farther apart, revealing a boulder behind them. The branches reshaped, creaking as they twisted up and around each other, meeting at the top to form a huge archway.

"The trees just moved." Chris drew back, his face pale. "They *moved*. Like they're alive."

"Trees *are* alive," Danielle said slowly. "But yeah, they moved. And trees don't do that."

"These trees do." I glanced at her and then back at where Kate stood, mesmerized, in front of the boulder.

"It looks like a door," Blake said, taking a step forward. "I would say we should go through it, but we can't walk through rock."

"True." I turned my attention back to Kate. "What did you mean that you were 'talking to the trees?'"

"I touched them and I could communicate with them." She shrugged. "In my head, of course. I can do that with all plants." She nodded, like that explained everything, and turned to Blake. "You're right—it's a door. We're supposed to walk through it."

"But it leads to a rock," he said again. "The 'door' doesn't go anywhere."

"Or it doesn't *look* like it goes anywhere."

Danielle laughed. "So we're supposed to walk through the boulder?" she asked. "And it's supposed to take us where? To a secret platform so we can board a magical train?"

I almost laughed as well, but then I saw Kate bite her lip like she was about to cry, and I stopped myself.

"If we go in there, we'll be able to get out, right?" Chris asked. "We won't get stuck on the other side?"

"There's only one way to know," Kate said. "Let's test it out."

Before any of us could stop her, she stepped into the rock, disappearing completely. Ripples spread across the granite, like when a stone is dropped into a pond.

I stared at the rock in disbelief. "Where did she go?" I asked. "Is she gone?"

"I don't know," Chris said. "Should one of us go in after her?"

We all continued staring at the boulder. No one volunteered.

"I can go," Blake stepped up, his face hard with determination.

"No." Danielle grabbed his hand, as if that would be enough to stop him. "Don't try to pull that again. Earth is Kate's element. She knows what she's doing. If you go after her, you might hurt yourself. Again."

"That's a risk we'll have to take." He pulled his hand out of hers and crossed his arms. "We can't just stand here doing nothing."

"I should be the one to do it," I said, wishing I could sound half as brave as Blake. "If Kate's hurt, I can heal her."

"You could ..." Danielle stared at me, her finger on her chin, as if she was sizing me up.

"You can't go alone." Blake locked his gaze with mine. "We'll both go."

I stepped closer to him, trying to swallow down the panic surging through my veins.

"Don't worry," he murmured, placing his hands on my shoulders. "I won't let anything bad happen to you. I promise."

I nodded and took a deep breath. Blake would keep me safe. I had to trust him.

But what if whatever was waiting on the other side of that rock was too dangerous for either of us to handle?

Before I could think about it too much, Kate stepped back out, a huge smile on her face. "See?" she said, brushing a twig out of her hair. "The trees don't lie."

"Thank God you're okay!" I exclaimed, running up to her and giving her a huge hug. "We had no idea where you'd gone. We were about to go in after you."

"I'm fine," she said with a small laugh. "Really. It's no big deal."

She did seem to be okay. Then I realized that I was about two feet away from the boulder, and I took a few steps back. The boulder probably couldn't suck us in, but it didn't hurt to be careful.

"I guess this means that if we go in, we can get back out," Blake said, joining Kate next to the boulder. "Good to know."

"But where does it lead?" Chris asked.

"I couldn't tell." Kate shrugged. "It was pitch black in there, but it smelled musty, like the Earth. Blake can use his fire power to light the way. But this is where we have to go next—I *know* it. So are you all coming or what?"

I stepped forward at the same time as Danielle. Kate made room for me between her and Blake, and Danielle stood on the other side of him. My fingers brushed against Blake's when I squeezed into my spot. The contact caused a wave of heat to course through my body, but I stuffed my hand into the front pocket of my jacket, not wanting to let Blake distract me from what we were about to do.

Chris trudged forward to stand next to Kate. "I guess I'm coming, too," he gave in, surveying the arching branches.

"Follow me." Kate squared her shoulders and reached her arm out, her hand sinking into the granite like it was no denser than the air. Then she closed her eyes and walked into the boulder, vanishing inside of it once again.

"I'm next." Blake walked into the rock like it was something he did every day, disappearing from sight.

I stepped forward, but Danielle's elbow pushed against my chest, blocking my way.

"I'm going after Blake." She flung her hair over her shoulder so it hit my face, and stepped through the boulder.

Chris was the only other one of us left. He shoved his hands into his pockets and shifted from one foot to the other. "After you," he said, motioning for me to go first.

The sparkling granite was inches from my face, and

I clenched my fists to my sides, unsure if I could do it. I trusted that Kate was telling us the truth that it was safe, but she didn't know the details of how this portal—or whatever it was—worked. What if she was the only one supposed to go through, and it shredded the rest of us into bits? Or what if we all got through in one piece, but ended up in different places?

But as terrified as I was, I also didn't want to be left alone in these woods. So I pushed the worry from my mind and closed my eyes, trying to relax. It would be easier to walk through solid granite if I didn't have to watch it approach.

Then I took a deep breath and stepped into the rock.

CHAPTER THIRTY-ONE

Walking through the boulder reminded me of one of those mist machines at theme parks—cold and prickly against my skin. The whooshing of the wind through the trees instantly disappeared. All I could hear now was the steady dripping of water echoing from the distance. Damp, musty air filled my nose, and the humidity layered on my skin—it was like I was in a windowless basement with a leaky pipe that hadn't been tended to in years.

Finally I opened my eyes. Kate, Blake, and Danielle stared back at me, and relief rushed through my veins at the sight of them.

Wherever we were was dark—the balls of fire in Blake's hands were the only light we had. Jagged, patchy shadows stretched across the ground, and I looked up to see what would cause shapes like that.

Huge stalactites dropped down from above, like they were defending the area against unwanted visitors. I was no geologist, but even though the ceiling was too high up to see in the darkness, there was no mistaking what this was.

We were in a cavern.

Air whooshed behind me, and Chris stepped through a shimmering wall. He stumbled forward and steadied himself. "That was easier than I thought," he said, blinking a few times and looking around. His voice echoed when he spoke, making him sound louder than normal. "We're in a cave. Cool."

"A huge cave," I added, still trying to figure out how big it was. Blake's fire didn't come close to filling it up, making it impossible to tell.

Danielle turned on her heel to look at Kate. "Do you know where the clue is?" she asked.

"No." Kate shook her head. "And the compass is useless. The arrow just keeps spinning around."

"So let's explore," Blake said, the flames in his hands growing taller. Without waiting for a reply, he turned and walked forward.

"Wait." Danielle held her hands up, stopping us. "We need to remember how to get back here. As far as we know, this door is our only way out, and we need to be able to find it. Does anyone have something we can use to mark our path?"

"Like how Hansel and Gretel used bread crumbs so they didn't get lost in the woods?" Kate asked.

"Yes," she said. "Exactly like that."

"I'll remember how to get back," I told her.

"But if your perfect sense of direction fails, or if we need to split up, we'll need a backup plan," Danielle said, lifting her chin defiantly in the air.

"Fine." I held my hands out in defeat. I doubted my new directional sense would suddenly stop working, and splitting up was rarely a good idea, but it wasn't worth arguing with Danielle.

She nodded, her expression serious. "Now, like I asked before, does anyone have anything to mark the path with?"

"The prophecy only took up a small part of the paper," I said, removing the crumpled sheet from my back pocket. "This is only a copy, so I can tear off the part with the writing on it and rip the rest to mark our path."

"Good idea," Blake said. "Chris—you stay in the back and drop pieces of paper behind you every ten feet or so. Make sure they're small. We don't want to run out."

"Sure thing," Chris said, although the frown on his face gave me the feeling that he wasn't happy about being stuck in back.

I tore off the part of the page that held the prophecy and handed the rest of the paper to Chris. The part with writing on it was so narrow that it looked like it could have come out of a giant fortune cookie. I folded it up and put it back into my pocket, taking a deep breath in preparation to explore the darkness ahead.

We only made it twenty feet, and then Blake

stopped in his path, holding his arms out to keep us from going any further.

CHAPTER THIRTY-TWO

Ahead of us, the ground came to a startling halt, dropping into the darkness with no end in sight.

"Don't get any closer," Blake said, throwing a ball of fire downward. It fell about a hundred feet, hit the ground, and sizzled out. I spotted what looked like a tunnel at the bottom, and then the light disappeared completely.

"Great," I mumbled, kicking a pebble over the edge. It clattered when it reached the ground. My head spun, and I took a step back so I wouldn't have to look anymore. "We walk for less than a minute and reach a cliff."

"Should we try going another way?" Chris asked.

"No." Blake threw another ball of fire, lighting up

the bottom once more. Again, it went out after a few seconds. "I can't keep the fire going from this far away, but there's a tunnel down there," he said. "We need to figure out how to get to it."

"No problem." Chris pushed up the sleeves of his jacket and looked down the cliff.

"Seriously?" Kate said. "You're going to float us all down? Do you have enough energy left to do that?"

"Easily." He rubbed his hands together, smiling and looking around at all of us. "Who wants to go first?"

"I'll go," Kate volunteered. "I already know what to do, since you flew me up to try getting the eagle. Not like you have to *do* anything," she assured us. "But at least I'm prepared."

"But what are we going to do about light?" Danielle asked. "Blake can't be in two places at once, and Chris needs to be able to see the person he's lowering down."

"She's right." Chris nodded. "If I can't see someone, I'll drop them."

"Can you hold two people at once?" Blake asked him.

"Probably," Chris said slowly. "As long as you stay close together."

"How about this," Blake said, glancing down the cliff. "I'll go down with one person and hold onto them to light the way. Then you bring me back up, and we'll continue like that until everyone is down."

"I think I can manage that." Chris looked down the cliff again, and then glanced at Kate. "You still up for going first?"

"Are you sure about this?" She didn't sound as

confident as she did a few minutes ago. I couldn't blame her, since Chris didn't sound positive that he could pull it off.

"Why don't I go first?" I volunteered. The words shocked me the moment I spoke them. But as much as I hated heights, I might as well get this over with. That way, I wouldn't have to stand up here freaking out for longer than necessary. "I'm the one with the healing ability, so if anyone falls and gets hurt, I can fix them."

"After how much you've already used your power today?" Blake shook his head. "Are you sure you can handle it?"

"I'll be fine," I said, even though he was right that I'd used my power a lot today. I didn't feel like I was about to pass out on the spot, but I did feel more tired than normal.

Hopefully everyone would get down in one piece and it wouldn't be an issue.

I glanced down the cliff again, my body shaking at the reminder of the height. A wave of dizziness overtook me, and I stepped back. "Are you ready?" I asked Chris, somehow managing to sound more confident than I felt.

Chris nodded. "Go stand next to Blake." He looked over at Blake, who was next to the ledge. "Don't drop her, or we won't have our healer."

"Don't worry," Blake said, looking at me. "I won't drop you." He held a hand out, focusing on me like he was trying to will me to believe him.

"I know you won't," I said, taking his hand. His

palm radiated warmth, most likely from the fire he'd held in it seconds before. He still held a ball of fire in his other hand. It glowed bright against his skin. My hands wouldn't stop shaking, and I tightened my grip around his to calm down. "I trust you."

He wrapped his arm around me, pulling me closer until my cheek rested against his chest. The warmth felt nice compared to the freezing cold we'd dealt with for the majority of the day. I held onto him tightly and took a deep breath. He smelled good—like a campfire on a summer night. He wasn't going to let me fall, and neither was Chris.

"Get ready." Chris's voice rang loudly in the cave. "I'm starting now."

The air swirled around me, pushing up against my feet. The ground floated away until Blake and I hovered inches away from the cliff. While I technically wasn't standing on anything, it felt like there was something beneath my feet—like the air had condensed so it could hold us, although it wasn't solid, either. It was like walking on a cloud.

The make-believe cloud moved to the side, bringing the two of us with it. Suddenly we were past the ledge, and the ground disappeared from under our feet. My pulse quickened. If Chris dropped us now, that would be it.

I squeezed my eyes shut, pressing my cheek against Blake's chest and listening to the steady beat of his heart. It kept my mind off the fact that I was floating down a hundred foot drop and could fall at any moment if Chris lost his concentration or sight of us.

My heart sped up at the thought, and my lungs squeezed together, suffocating me until all I could manage were short, shallow breaths.

Blake's arm tightened around my waist, holding me closer. "Are you okay?" he whispered, soft enough so no one else could hear.

"I'm fine," I lied. "Are we almost there?"

"Just a few feet more." The warmth of the nearby fire let me know that I wasn't totally surrounded by darkness, which allowed me to breathe easier. Of course we were going to be fine. Chris wouldn't let us fall.

After what felt like forever, my feet finally touched the ground. Once sure I was steady, I willed myself to open my eyes. A rock wall greeted me. I looked up, unable to make out the shapes of the others at the top of the cliff.

"Are you guys all right?" Chris called down.

"We're good," Blake answered, his arm still tight around my waist. Neither of us made an effort to move away from one another. "You did a great job," he said, soft enough that only I could hear.

Then everything went dark. It was pitch black, and not like when it's night time and the stars and moon are shining overhead so you can still tell where you are. It was like I'd gone blind. I held my hand in front of my face to test if I could see it, but it made no difference. The entire world had disappeared.

"What's going on down there?" Chris screamed from up in the darkness.

"The fire went out and I dropped my lighter," Blake

said. "Hold on while I find it."

"Is everything okay?" I asked, quieter, so only he could hear. "Are you tired from using your powers so much today? If you need a break, I'm sure everyone would wait."

"I'm fine," he said. "Although it's sweet that you're so worried."

"Okay." I struggled to see, but it was impossible. All I could focus on was the pressure of Blake's arm still wrapped tightly around my waist, and that we were standing so close that I could feel his breath on my cheek.

He moved to face me, his nose brushing mine. "Do you want to know a secret?" he asked.

"What secret?" I asked, my voice barely louder than a whisper.

"The fire didn't go out by accident."

Then he pressed his lips to mine, and the world disappeared around me. He traced his fingers up my arm, and before I knew what was happening, he'd pinned me against the wall of the cliff, his fingers entangled deep into my hair. My hand found its way to his, our palms connecting. A wave of energy passed through my body as the bond between us twisted together, reminding me of what I'd felt earlier while healing him.

We shouldn't be doing this—but I didn't care. All that mattered was Blake kissing me, and how I never wanted him to stop.

"What's taking so long down there?" Chris's voice jolted me back into reality—the reality where Danielle was standing a hundred feet above, blinded to how her boyfriend was cheating on her under her nose.

Guilt flooded my chest, and I pulled away from Blake, glad that it was too dark for us to see each other. Otherwise he would see the hold he had over me, and it would make it harder for me to do what was right.

"I dropped the lighter and had to find it," Blake called back. "I got it now."

"Good," Danielle said, and at the sound of her voice, I took another step away from Blake. If I didn't, I was afraid I would reach for him again, and I couldn't allow that to happen. "Can you put it back on?" she asked. "It's pitch dark in here."

"Yeah," Blake said. "Just a moment."

His hand brushed mine, but I pulled away, running my fingers through my hair to smooth it. My stomach twisted with the knowledge of what I'd let happen. Contributing to cheating was unlike me. Then again, I wasn't the same person as I was back in Georgia. Now I knew that the blood of ancient gods runs through my veins, and that I have powers most people don't believe exist.

But I wouldn't let that change my morals. Because despite what Blake had told me about wanting to end his relationship with Danielle, he hadn't done it yet.

Until he did, nothing could happen between us.

"Nicole?" he whispered. "Are you okay?"

"That never should have happened," I said. "It can't happen again."

"You don't mean that."

"Yes." I swallowed away tears. "I do. Now, go get the others. They're waiting."

He was silent for a few seconds, as if expecting me to take it back. But I didn't. So he flicked the lighter back on, and despite being able to see again, I refused to meet his gaze. Because if I did, I might lose it completely.

CHAPTER THIRTY-THREE

It didn't take Chris long to lower Kate, Danielle, and himself down the cliff. I couldn't look at Blake again, for fear that one of the others would see the way I was looking at him and realize that something had happened between us in the darkness. It was the hardest when he brought down Danielle, his arms wrapped tightly around her the same way they'd been around me. Because despite what he'd told me about wanting to break up with her, they had history together. They'd known each other for *years*. How was I supposed to compete with that?

Not wanting to focus on them for fear of tearing up again, I looked around to get an idea of my surroundings. The cavern looked even bigger from the bottom of the cliff than from the top. The walls sloped up into a dome, the stalagmites and stalactites growing longer down here than the ones on the top of the cliff. Some of them were so old that they now met together to form giant columns.

"Let's keep going," Blake said, turning around to continue forward.

We reached the end of the room and arrived at the tunnel we'd seen from the top of the cliff. It was about ten feet tall, like a gaping mouth, and like the rest of the cavern, it was so dark that I couldn't see where it led. A warm breeze blew from inside of it, pushing a few strands of my hair out of place. It was like the place was alive. And while I didn't know what was waiting at the end, I had a terrible feeling about it.

"We're really supposed to go in *there*?" I asked. "What if it collapses on us?"

"I have power over the earth," Kate said. "I won't let that happen."

I nodded and tried to swallow down my worry. We couldn't turn back now. And Kate was right. We all had powers over the elements, and we wouldn't let anything happen to each other. I had to trust my friends.

"I'll go first and light the way," Blake said, taking a few steps closer to the opening, the fire glowing brightly in his hands.

I hurried to follow him, but Danielle had the same idea, and I nearly crashed into her. She glared at me and scurried ahead so she was directly behind Blake. Kate walked behind me, and Chris trailed in the back.

He diligently dropped a piece of paper every so often to mark our path.

Blake's light didn't extend far enough to show us an end anywhere in sight. We continued forward, the air thickening with humidity. Beads of sweat accumulated along my brow, and I unzipped my coat, which was a welcome change from the freezing weather we'd had outside.

A feint bubbling echoed in the distance, like water in a pot when it starts to boil. Finally the tunnel came to an end and dumped us into another large chamber.

The fire in Blake's hand grew bigger. "We have another problem," he said, his voice steady as he looked straight ahead.

The ground ended, but this time it didn't stop at a cliff. It met with a steaming lake of boiling water that spread the entire width of the cave. Huge bubbles popped to the surface, and it was so hot and sticky in the chamber that I wanted to peel off every layer I was wearing and toss it on the ground. Instead, I pulled my hair back into a ponytail, grateful for the hairband I always kept on my wrist.

"Do you think you can fly us across?" I asked Chris.

"I used a lot of my energy up back at the cliff," he said. "I wish I could say yes. But really … I don't know."

I glanced across the cave again in defeat. The only way to the other side was to swim. Unfortunately, that would be impossible without burning ourselves to death. And my healing power wouldn't do any good if we couldn't make it across alive.

"Why do you all look like the world's about to end?" Danielle laughed and stepped to the ledge. "It's just a boiling lake. I've got this." She tossed her hair over her shoulder and kneeled down, lowering her hand into the water. I expected her to scream in pain, but she just squeezed her eyes shut, bracing herself as she focused on whatever she was trying to do.

A cracking sound filled the cavern, and a thick line of water turned into ice, forming a path that led straight to the other side. The lake boiled around it, but the path didn't melt.

"See?" Danielle flung the water off her hands and smiled. "No problem. I don't know why you all doubt my powers so much."

"Hopefully none of us slip while walking across," Kate said, her lower lip trembling as she looked at the path.

Chris moved next to her and placed a hand on her shoulder. "Take your time," he told her, his voice soft and reassuring. "I'll be right behind you."

"Thanks." Kate leaned into him and took a deep breath.

Blake placed one foot gently against the ice and put some pressure on it. It seemed solid, and he put his other foot down, too, so he stood completely on top of it.

"It holds," he said, bouncing his knees to test it out further. "Just remember to take it slow. If you rush, you'll risk slipping and falling in."

Kate looked over at Danielle, who was smiling as she admired her work. "I don't know why you didn't freeze the whole lake," Kate muttered, loud enough to be heard over the boiling water.

"Stop complaining," Danielle said. "I've used up a lot of energy today. It would take about a hundred times more energy to freeze the whole lake, and I didn't want to risk it. I can do more if it's too hard for you, but the path is wide enough that I don't see why it would be a problem." She spun around and strutted towards the lake, digging her stilettos into the ground for emphasis.

"It's easy for her to say," Kate spoke softly enough so only Chris and I could hear. "She won't boil to death if she falls in."

"You're not going to fall in," I assured her, even though looking at the bubbling water surrounding the ice path made me uneasy, too. "Take it slow and you'll be fine. On the off-chance that anyone *does* fall in, I can heal them."

As long as we pulled them out before they boiled to death.

She nodded, and I headed toward the path, watching Blake and Danielle as they made their way across. They made it look so easy. I put one foot on the ice, and it wasn't as slippery as I'd anticipated. Even so, I took each step slowly, not wanting to lose my footing. It wasn't too hard—as long as I focused on my feet and didn't look at the boiling water on both sides of me.

Danielle and Blake stood halfway across the path, waiting for us to catch up. I reached them, and glanced over my shoulder to see how Kate and Chris were progressing.

Kate was only about a quarter of the way down the path. She trembled before each step, holding her arms out at both sides to balance herself. Chris stood behind her, his hands poised to catch her if she fell.

They eventually made it to us, and Blake turned to lead the way down the remaining part of the path. The first half hadn't been too hard. We could do this.

He and Danielle easily made it to the other end in the amount of time that it took me to travel ten feet. Reminding myself that I only had a little farther to go, I took another step forward, focusing on staying steady and not slipping.

Then something cracked from behind.

I glanced over my shoulder, and my heart leaped into my throat at what I saw. The ice at the beginning of the path had cracked. It crumbled into the boiling water, melting on impact. Another chunk fell in a second later. At this pace, it wouldn't be long until it caught up with us.

Terrified, I turned back around and ran. It was slippery, and despite almost losing my footing a few times, I kept my balance and made it to the other side. My body wouldn't stop shaking, and I wrapped my arms around myself, breathing steady and focusing on collecting blue energy to calm down.

Once relaxed, I looked back at Kate and Chris. Kate was ahead of Chris, and she was taking each step slowly, her eyes wide in fear. The ice melted behind them, catching up quickly—they wouldn't make it in time. And if I ran back onto the path to help them, it would only take up space and create more chaos. I could crash into them, or fall in.

They had to hurry and make it on their own.

"Grab her and fly yourselves across!" I screamed to Chris.

"I don't have enough energy left." He buried his fingers in his hair, sweat dripping down his face. "Not after sending everyone down the cliff. Come on, Kate. You have to run."

"You just have to make it to my hand." Blake stepped to the edge, reaching his arm forward. "Then I'll pull you in."

Danielle crouched next to the lake, her hand emerged in the boiling water, her eyes squeezed shut. The path was melting faster now. It was getting dangerously close to Chris, who looked like he was about to pick Kate up and carry her across himself. Kate glanced behind her, saw how quickly the ice was disappearing, and hurried towards us, her eyes wide in panic.

She almost made it, but her foot slipped from under her and sent her toppling towards the ice. I held my breath, frozen in fear, unable to do anything to help.

Then Chris reached forward and grabbed her from under her arms. He caught her right before she could roll over the edge. They collapsed into a heap on the path, steady for now.

But the ice was still melting, and it wouldn't be long until it caught up with them. What was taking Danielle so long to stop it? She remained still as she concentrated, her head bowed towards the water, her hand submerged within it.

Finally the ice stopped crumbling, inches before it reached Kate and Chris.

Kate pushed herself up to sitting position and pulled her legs towards her chest. All of the color had drained from her face. Chris reached down and scooped her into his arms, somehow keeping his balance while carrying her to the end of the lake.

"That was close," he said, placing Kate on the ground. His cheeks were bright red, and he rested his hands on his knees, breathing heavily.

Kate scrambled away and braced herself against the wall. "Remind me to never do that again." She shook her head and looked out at the lake, which had returned to its natural boiling state.

I wished I could promise her that, but I couldn't. Because we would likely have to come back the way we came. And we'd used up so much of our energy making it this far ... how were we supposed to make it back?

But we were already here, so I couldn't worry about that now. We had to focus on what was coming next. Because looming ahead was another tunnel, identical to the one we'd faced at the bottom of the cliff.

We had no other option but to continue forward.

CHAPTER THIRTY-FOUR

This tunnel was shorter than the first—so short that we could see the light at the other end. Even from far away I could make out the shapes of candles lining the sides of the walls. At least Blake wouldn't have to use his power to keep it lit anymore.

I stepped inside the next chamber, and froze at what I saw.

My sister was on a wooden chair in the center of the room, her wrists and feet bound together, her arms tied behind her. A cloth was wrapped around her mouth so she couldn't speak. She squirmed in place, her curly hair huge and messy, as if she'd gotten in a fight.

"Becca!" I ran towards her and ungagged her,

checking her for injuries. Other than the raw red areas where the rope had rubbed against her skin, there didn't appear to be anything seriously wrong with her, which was a huge relief. But her involvement in this made no sense. "What on Earth is going on?"

Her mouth opened like she was about to say something, but nothing came out. For the first time in her life, Becca was speechless.

I kneeled down to undo the knots around her wrists, tugging at the rope as hard as possible. But it refused to budge. Then Kate screamed my name, and I turned to see what she wanted.

A shadow passed over the floor, and an oversized bird landed next to me with a resonating boom, its huge feathery wing pushing me over. My elbow collided with the ground and broke the fall, cracking on impact. I immediately grabbed it and healed it.

Once the pain resided, I could focus on what had pushed me in the first place.

I saw the claws first—huge crooked orange things with three toes each. They looked like bird feet, but mutated to five times the size. The orange ribbed skin climbed up to the middle of the creature's thighs, where it changed into human-looking flesh. Its arms were similar—its hands talons, morphing into regular-looking skin around the elbow. Red wings jutted out of its back, spanning about six feet each. Wrinkles covered the skin on its face, like an old woman who had spent too much time in the sun, and a huge hooked beak sat where its mouth should have been.

Its features looked female, but all I knew was that it

wasn't human.

It stared down at me with its huge yellow eyes and sauntered towards me, letting out a cackle and throwing its head back. I scooted back and looked around, but there was nothing I could use to defend myself. I was trapped.

Then a ball of fire whizzed through the air, hitting it straight in the wing. Blake stood a few feet behind it, holding his lighter in his hand and preparing to launch another fireball.

The creature turned around and hissed at him. "I don't want to fight with you," it said through its pointed beak, shocking me with the fact that it could talk. Its voice was hoarse, like it hadn't spoken in years, and it patted down its wing to put out the fire. Tendrils of smoke rose up toward the ceiling, and the tips of its feathers had been singed to a dark charcoal. "I simply want to discuss a deal," it continued. "Once we make the exchange, you're all free to leave."

"My sister, too?" I asked, resting a hand on the back of her chair.

"She's part of the deal," the creature hissed. It tucked its wings closer to its sides, the smell of burnt feathers lingering in the air. "Now, are you ready to listen?"

I looked over at the others. They had spread out in a semi-circle at the entrance of the chamber. Blake gripped his lighter, ready to fight. Chris and Danielle held their hands out as well.

"We'll listen," Kate said, her voice surprisingly calm. "But that doesn't mean we'll agree."

Blake lowered his lighter, and Chris and Danielle relaxed their stances. Now that I wasn't trying to free my sister or run away from the creature, I was able to take in more of the chamber. The front wall shimmered, similar to the boulder in the woods that had led us into the cavern. On the back wall, a murky, muddy substance swirled in the shape of a door. Looking at it made my stomach drop, like it had when I first glimpsed Bosley Woods.

When it was clear that no one was going to attack, the creature said, "Behind me, you'll find the Book of Shadows." It moved to the side, and I saw an elegant, wooden stand balancing an ancient-looking book. A few feet behind it was another cliff.

"The Book of Shadows," Kate repeated, her lips parted in awe. "*That's* what the prophecy meant by 'the Shadows.' We were being led to the Book this entire time."

"The Book is what I assumed you came here for," the creature said. "Which means you are the five from the prophecy who are gifted with powers over the elements."

"We go by the Elementals," Chris chimed in, forcing a half-smile. Danielle nudged him with her elbow in a silent plea to be quiet.

If the creature had irises in the center of its yellow eyes, I swear it would have rolled them. "Right." It focused on me, and I shuddered under its gaze. "Here's the deal I'm willing to propose. You give me the Book in exchange for your sister. Then all of you can go."

"Why don't you grab the Book yourself?" I squared

my shoulders, hoping I looked more confident than I felt.

"Because the one with the power of spirit is the only one who can lift it from the podium." The creature snarled, raising its wings into an arc above its head. "I sent the stupid hound Orthrus to fetch you, but apparently that wasn't enough. Now, hand me the Book, and I'll let your sister go instead of throwing her into Kerberos." It glanced at the muddy door, and I realized—that portal led to Kerberos. That was the prison world Darius had mentioned in class, where all of the evil creatures who'd rebelled against the Olympians had been contained.

Wasn't the portal to Kerberos supposed to be sealed forever?

"How did you get Becca here in the first place?" I asked, crossing my arms over my chest. Stalling the creature would buy us time. It was all I could think to do right now.

"The portal has been weakened, and a few of us have been able to escape," it said, pulling its wings back to its sides. "After my unsuccessful attempt to send the hound Orthrus to fetch you, I decided to do it myself. But this time I went after easier prey—your sister. I brought her here a few hours ago. After you left on your scavenger hunt with your friends, it was easy to get through the second floor window of your house to capture her. Your mom's music was playing so loudly that she didn't even hear her scream." The creature glared at me, and I gripped my sister's chair tighter. "But the choice is yours," it continued. "If you refuse to hand over the Book, the energy of six witches will make my friends in there very happy." It pointed a talon at the muddy door—the portal to Kerberos—and cackled again.

It doesn't know that Becca's not a witch, I realized.

Danielle stepped forward and stuck her chin in the air. "What's to stop you from throwing us in there even if Nicole gives you the Book?" she asked.

"Just my word." It smiled to the best of its ability given that it had a beak instead of a mouth.

"Because that's *so* reliable." Becca sneered.

The creature raised a talon and hissed at her. Then it turned its hungry eyes back at me. "My word is all you have to go on," it said. "And you're not exactly in the position to bargain. So ... what's it going to be?"

CHAPTER THIRTY-FIVE

I stared into the creature's yellow eyes, trying not to fidget—even though it could rip me apart in a minute without breaking a sweat. It let out a low hiss, and I knew I had to do something. It wasn't going to wait all day.

I marched towards the Book and held my hands above it like I was preparing to lift it from the stand. Then I looked at Blake and nodded.

He flicked on his lighter and threw a fireball at the creature, hitting the side of its face. It opened its beak and let out a head-splitting squawk.

"That's right," Blake said, his eyes charged with anger. "Your word means nothing." He threw another fireball at its chest, but the creature opened its wings and flew through the air, landing near Kate. The flames hit the rock wall and fizzled out on impact.

Kate froze and backed towards the wall. The creature towered over her, tilting back its head and cackling.

"Over here!" Chris yelled, raising his hands frantically above his head. A gust of air collided with the creature, slamming it against the wall. It snarled, shook itself off, and charged towards him. Its claws struck the ground with enough force to shake the cavern.

Blake threw another fireball at its wings, at the same time that Chris pushed his arms forward, sending another rush of air into the creature's chest. The creature crashed into the wall, inches away from the muddy portal to Kerberos. Its wings blazed from the fire, and it rolled onto the ground to put it out, thick smoke swirling around it.

Blake and Chris inched closer towards it, continuing to attack it with their powers. I kneeled down next to Becca, who was struggling to free herself from the ropes.

"What *is* that thing?" she asked, her voice coming out in tiny gasps. "And how are you all doing this superpower stuff?"

"I'll explain later," I told her, pulling at the ropes around her wrists. "Stop struggling so I can get you out of this."

She did as I said, but the knots were so tight that no matter how hard I pulled, they wouldn't come undone. Her wrists had been rubbed so raw that they were bleeding. Her blood was smeared all over my hands. I closed my eyes and called on white energy, healing her before continuing with my attempts to get her untied. But as hard as I tried, I couldn't loosen the ropes. I needed Blake's firepower to burn them away, but he was busy defending us against the creature.

Then I saw someone move in the corner of my eye—Danielle. She stood in front of the tunnel, her arms raised in the air. Before I could figure out what she doing, water streamed inside from the opening, hitting the creature in the chest and sizzling on impact. It must have been the boiling water from the nearby chamber.

The creature arched its head back and let out a screech so loud that it felt like my eardrums were about to burst. Blake threw a ball of fire at its exposed neck, and it squawked again, stumbling backward and collapsing in a heap against the wall. Its lifeless wings flopped to its sides.

Silence filled the chamber for the first time since we'd entered.

"Did you kill it?" Kate asked, backing up to the wall.

"Maybe." Chris took a few steps forward. "Who wants to check?"

Blake created two more fireballs and threw them at its chest. "Just to be safe," he explained.

But the creature's yellow eyes snapped open, and it let out another screech, lifting its wings into an arc above its head. It scrambled onto its feet and spun on its claw to face me, its eyes burning with anger as it stared me down.

Then it charged.

I hurried away from Becca, and a few balls of fire whizzed past me, so close that I could feel the heat on my face. Someone yelled my name seconds before the mass of feathers collided with my body. The force of the creature's weight pushed me backwards, towards the cliff I'd noticed earlier, and the ground disappeared beneath my feet. I reached blindly for something to hold onto, and a scream that I vaguely recognized as my own echoed through the cavern.

Then my head collided with the ground, and everything went dark.

CHAPTER THIRTY-SIX

My skull felt like it had shattered, the tiny pieces lodged into the crevices of my brain. I managed to open my eyes, but the world spun so quickly that I had to shut them again to stop myself from being sick. The pounding in my head was a deafening beat in my mind. It was like someone had taken a gong, placed it next to my ear, and was hitting it as hard as they could with the heaviest mallet they could find.

I lifted my arm to try to quiet the noise, but a sharp pain shot up from my elbow to my shoulder, so excruciating that it traveled through my entire body. The arm flopped uselessly to the ground. The impact sent another jolt of pain through my spine. My hair felt matted with something warm and sticky, and even though I couldn't move to touch it, I knew it was blood. I felt it dripping down my neck.

An ear-splitting scream echoed from above, and someone shouted my name. It was a muffled noise hidden behind the pounding that consumed my thoughts. I tried to open my eyes again, but I couldn't. Instead, yellow eyes burned in my mind, followed by a rush of red. Red, all around me. So much that I was drowning in it.

Then I thought about another color—white. White would make the pain end.

If only the pounding in my head would stop, so I could focus.

Another muffled scream echoed from above, followed by a thump as something crashed to the ground. The scream sounded like Kate, but I couldn't be sure.

Focus, I told myself, squeezing my eyes together as if it could make the pain disappear. *I can heal myself. I've done it before.*

But just because I could fix cuts and scratches didn't mean I could repair the damage from a fall off a cliff—especially given how much I'd already used my power today. What if I depleted my energy? I could die.

The thought terrified me. I knew that what we were going into today could be dangerous, but I didn't realize I might not survive it. Now, I was bleeding out at the bottom of a cliff. My friends were in danger, and it was very possible that they wouldn't be able to get to me in time. Even if they did, they couldn't do anything to help me, and we were still deep down in this cavern with no easy escape.

But if I didn't heal myself, I would definitely die. So despite the possibility of depleting my energy, I had to at least try.

I cleared my head as much as possible and closed my eyes, grasping for the energy around me. At first it didn't come. But I reached farther—so much that my head felt like it was about to explode from the effort—until finding it. It filled the cave like electricity, bouncing off the walls from every direction. I pulled it towards me, refusing to let it go until the streams of white entered my palms.

It hummed all around me, surrounding me in a cocoon of pure, crackling energy, soaking through my skin like water on a sponge. It was everywhere at once—inside and outside my body, leaving no part of me untouched. My surroundings melted around me until I had no idea where I was anymore. It was like floating inside a warm, white cloud that I could bend to my will.

Then the energy disappeared, the pain leaving with it. I could feel the ground beneath me again. I lifted my arm, anticipating another jolt of agonizing pain, but it moved normally, as though never injured to begin with. I touched the back of my head where I'd felt the blood earlier, and while the blood was still there, I couldn't find a wound.

I'd done it. My entire body had been broken, and I'd healed it all.

I opened my eyes, and the stalagmites and stalactites sharpened into focus, no longer a dizzying blur of shapes. The top of the cliff wasn't even that far away—maybe a six-foot drop.

I glanced around, trying to come up with a plan. Because when I made it back up the cliff, I would need to defend myself. But a cave didn't have as many possibilities for fighting materials as a playground. There were only the walls, the ground, and ... the stalactites and stalagmites.

If I could dislodge one, it would make a perfect stake.

I pulled at the one closest to me, but it didn't budge. I wasn't strong enough. I needed Kate and her earth power to pull a stalagmite from the ground. And judging by what I'd heard from the fight up there, she was in no position to help me.

Then a particularly sharp stalagmite caught my eye—it was thin and about the same length as a sword. I crawled over to it as silently as possible, trying to ignore the fire, rushes of water, gusts of wind, and screaming from above. All I could do was focus on what I could do to help, and that was in dislodging a stalagmite that was permanently attached to the ground. It was an impossible task, but I could do impossible things.

I just had to figure out *how*.

Then I remembered what I'd done in homeroom with the glass—when I'd made it explode by touching it with orange energy. If I could do the same thing with the stalagmite, maybe it could come loose. I would have to focus the energy on the exact right spot at the bottom of the stalagmite, to disconnect it without blowing the whole thing up. There was so much chaos up above that they wouldn't even hear it if I managed to succeed.

I inched closer to the stalagmite, crawling on my hands and knees, the world spinning with each movement. I had to stop a few times to catch my breath, but finally I made it. Now I had to focus on the energy. But when I tried, it was like I'd run into a wall. A rush of dizziness passed through my head, so intense that I had to lean back on my hands to steady myself. It was like I hadn't slept in days. It was tempting to lie on the ground and shut my eyes for a few minutes, but I listened to the screaming above, forced my eyes to stay open, and focused.

The energy continued to resist my pull. I was too exhausted. I couldn't do it. I closed my eyes, but then another shriek echoed through the cavern—Becca. Hearing her terror jolted me awake. My friends could defend themselves against the creature, but Becca was helpless. She shouldn't have been dragged into this.

I had to save her.

I focused on harnessing the energy, picturing orange around me until it surrounded every inch of my skin. I called on it on until my body felt so full of light that I couldn't collect any more. Then I touched the base of the stalagmite, narrowed my eyes, and sent the energy outwards in a single stream.

The stalagmite exploded with a giant crack.

Dust rose up, and I feared that I'd shattered it. But once it settled, I saw the stalagmite on the ground, fully intact. I reached for it, hoping it wouldn't crumble, relieved when it stayed in one piece. I wrapped my hand around it to get a firmer grip, and simply holding it made me feel more focused and awake.

I could do this.

But first I needed to get out of this ditch. I examined my surroundings to figure out how. The cliff wasn't a straight drop—there were places where rocks were piled beneath it. If I could get my footing and gather enough strength, I could hoist myself up. And so, I crawled to the largest rock and pulled myself on top of it, peering over the ledge to see what was happening above.

Blake and Danielle were attacking the bird-creature full-force with fire and scalding water, although their powers were weakening. The bird screeched in pain, although it continued moving towards them. Their only option was to back away, allowing it to corner them until they were trapped. Chris was guarding Becca, who was still tied to the chair, and Kate was nowhere to be seen.

It was now or never.

Gripping the stalagmite, I gathered enough energy to lift myself onto the ledge. But it took a lot of out me, and the dizziness hit me again. I took a few deep breaths to center myself. In this condition, there was no way I could aim as well as I'd done on the playground when I'd flung the monkey bar at the hound. And I only had one chance, since the creature's back was toward me. If I threw the stalagmite and missed, it would know I'd survived, and

I would lose the element of surprise. I had to do this on the first shot.

So I held out the stalagmite and sprinted towards the creature, staking its back and sinking the weapon deep into its skin.

CHAPTER THIRTY-SEVEN

The creature arched its neck and stumbled backward, shrieking and raising its wings in the air. I let go of the stalagmite, my eyes glued to the place where it was lodged between its wings.

I must have missed its heart, because it spun around and snarled. "You," it said, its throaty voice barely louder than a whisper. "That fall should have killed you. How did you get back up here?" It lifted one claw and took a small step towards me, its yellow eyes flashing in pain. Its face muscles tightened as it dragged the other claw forward to join the first. Grunting from the effort, the creature reached an arm around its back to find the stalagmite. It gripped it with its talons and yanked it out.

It opened its beak and let out an agonizing screech, dropping the weapon onto the ground. Scarlet blood dripped from the wound, collecting in a puddle below.

Chris didn't waste a second before blowing a gust of wind in the creature's direction. The force of it toppled the creature to the side, crushing one of its wings beneath its weight. Its head cracked when it hit the ground. I shuddered at the sound. But it forced opened its eyes, their yellow glow dimmed significantly, and kept its gaze locked on mine.

I stared it down, bending my knees in preparation to bolt if it got back up. "The fall didn't kill me," I finally answered its question. "I used my element to heal myself."

"You're stronger than I realized." Its words came out slowly, each syllable strained with effort. "But this is only the beginning. There are others trapped in Kerberos who are many times more powerful than me, and it won't be long until the portal weakens enough so they can break free, too. You'll have tough luck beating them based on what you showed me tonight." The creature paused, its labored breaths gurgling as it struggled to speak again. "Even the gods won't be able to save you once Typhon escapes and returns to his true form. I'll see you in Hades, my little demigod. And once Typhon rises, I'll be sure he gives you a one-way ticket to Tartarus."

It let out another strangled laugh, its breathing labored. Then, struck with a crazy idea, I stepped forward, pressing my palm to its chest. If I could heal with a touch, maybe I could do the opposite, too. Kill.

When I healed, I needed white energy. So when I destroyed, it made sense to use the opposite.

Black energy.

Except I didn't know how to channel black energy. I only knew about its existence—I'd never asked how to use it.

So I did the only thing that felt natural—I thought about hate. I *hated* this creature. It had kidnapped my sister. It was attacking my friends. It tried to *kill* me. It pushed me off that cliff and left me to die. If I hadn't healed myself and climbed back up here, it would have killed my friends. My sister, too.

The black energy swirled inside me, like pools of ink streaming through my veins, until there was so much of it that I couldn't contain it any longer. But I couldn't risk losing control of this dark energy and having it fill the cave. Who knew what would happen then? It was now or never.

So I stared into the creature's huge eyes and shot the darkness straight into its heart.

CHAPTER THIRTY-EIGHT

The creature let out a whoosh of breath, then it flickered and disappeared into the darkness. The only evidence that it had been there at all was the puddle of blood on the ground and the stained stalagmite lying next to it.

I stared at the place where it had been in shock. Had I really killed that thing? By just *touching* it?

"Are you just going to stand there, or are you going to heal Kate?" Danielle's question brought me back to reality.

"Kate?" I asked. "What happened to her? Where is she?"

Danielle glanced at the entrance to the chamber. "Behind you."

I turned to look, gasping at what I saw. Kate lay crumpled on the ground, with her back against the wall. She was so pale. Her hair draped over her face, partially covering her closed eyes, her arms splayed out beside her.

I hurried towards her, ignoring the fogginess seeping into my head with each step. "Kate?" I said her name softly, gently shaking her shoulder. I prayed that she'd open her eyes or twitch her fingers—something to show that she was alive. But she was completely still.

I reached for her wrist, letting out a long breath when I felt a pulse.

"Nicole?" Blake lowered himself to kneel next to me, placing his hand on my shoulder. "Are you sure you can heal her after all the energy you've already used today?"

"No," I said, the word dry in my throat. "But I have to try."

"You don't have enough energy left," Danielle said. "If you try this, you could kill yourself."

I swallowed, since it was likely that Danielle was right. "I know," I said, barely louder than a whisper. "But I can't let Kate die."

"We can all help you," Blake said. "Let us hold one of your hands. Then you can channel our energy and use your other hand to heal Kate."

"You won't be putting yourselves in danger?" I fought off another round of dizziness, and wiped a bead of sweat from my brow. "You've used a lot of energy today, too."

"We'll be fine." Blake's strong response made it clear that the offer wasn't up for debate. "We won't give you all of our energy. Just enough to help you save Kate."

"And do I have to ... do anything?" I asked. "To make it work?"

"Do what you normally do and pretend we aren't here." His eyes darkened, and he leaned so close to me that our faces were inches apart. "But remember that you're *channeling* our energy. Don't try to *take* it. Promise me you won't allow that to happen."

I looked back down at Kate. Her body remained still, her breaths shallow. Her face was growing paler by the second.

"I can do that," I said. "I promise."

"If you're doing this, I guess you could use my help, too," Danielle reluctantly said from behind me. Her gaze was hard, and despite not seeming thrilled about it, she knelt next to Blake. Chris joined, too, the three of them creating a semi-circle around me.

I held Kate's hand tighter in mine. It felt so fragile, like if I squeezed too hard all of the bones in it would shatter. Blake, Danielle, and Chris placed their hands on top of my other one, and a warm light rushed through my body. The fuzziness in my head disappeared, like someone had removed cotton balls from inside of my ears. Every sound around me became clearer—feet shuffling, water dripping from somewhere in the distance, and the buzz of energy pulsing through the air.

"Okay," I whispered, looking down at Kate. "This better work."

I prepared myself for the exertion it was bound to take after how much I'd already done that day, but calling forth the white energy wasn't nearly as hard as I'd expected. It clearly had something to do with the other three helping me, but I remembered what Blake had said and didn't focus on them. Instead, I thought about the white energy flowing through my body, from my head all the way down to my toes. It gathered together, entwined with lines of blue, red, and yellow, and grew outwards to the edges of my skin. When it felt like I could burst from the pressure of it all, I allowed it to stream out of my palms and into Kate's.

The energy whooshed out of my body as quickly as air coming out of a balloon. Once it was gone, I opened my eyes and squeezed Kate's hand tighter, as if doing so would have an impact on whether or not she'd be okay.

She still didn't move.

Then, just when I thought that what I'd done hadn't been enough, her eyes fluttered open.

She looked at me first, then at Blake, Danielle, and Chris. Her eyes didn't shine with the same brightness as usual, but at least she was alive.

"What happened?" Her voice was barely louder than a whisper. "Did you guys kill the harpy?"

"The what?" I asked, sitting back on my heels.

"The harpy." She shook her head and sat up, resting against the wall. "The thing that looked like a cross-breed between an old woman and a mutated bird. They're in charge of bringing the unwilling to Tartarus. Some of them supported the Titans in the

Second Rebellion, so those harpies were sent to Kerberos."

Leave it to Kate to give me a history lesson immediately after returning from the brink of death.

Chris took his hand off of mine and scooted closer to Kate. "You bet we killed it," he said with a laugh. "The three of us injured it pretty badly, and Nicole finished it off with a stalagmite. It was pretty awesome." He held a pretend stalagmite in the air and jammed it forward to reenact the attack. "Then it disappeared..." he trailed off, his eyes distant. "I don't know where it went. But it's gone now."

I glanced back at the bloody stalagmite. My head spun with the movement, my stomach swirling with nausea. Chris didn't realize that I'd killed the harpy with a touch. He thought it was because of the stalagmite.

Could that be what they *all* thought? Maybe I should let them continue believing that, and not tell them the truth. Kate had told me on my first day here that using black energy was illegal. I didn't know why—I didn't even know what black energy was typically used for. But I did know that what I'd done could get me in trouble with the Elders ... perhaps so much that they would take away my powers.

And what if I told my friends the truth and it scared them too much? What if they thought I was some sort of monster?

It might be best not to risk it.

"Now that you're finished whatever it is you're doing over there, can someone please get me out of this chair?" Becca's shrill voice filled the chamber, yanking me out of my thoughts.

How had I gotten so distracted with saving Kate that I hadn't remembered to untie Becca? At least she didn't appear to have any injuries besides a few cuts. The bird-woman—harpy—must have been so focused on defending itself against the others that it didn't have time to do anything more to Becca.

"I've got it." Chris jumped up and ran over to Becca. He fiddled with the ropes, untying the ones around her wrists and starting on the ones around her ankles.

I was glad he volunteered, because my head felt hazy again, and I had to struggle to keep my eyes open, like I hadn't slept in days. I pulled my legs to my chest and buried my head in my knees. I would be fine. I *had* to be fine. I just needed a few minutes to rest.

"Nicole?" Blake asked, holding me steady. "Are you okay?"

"I'm just tired," I mumbled, forcing my eyes open in an attempt to remain awake.

Becca ran towards me before Blake could say anything more, wrapping her arms around me with so much force that she nearly pushed me to the ground. "What was that thing?" she asked, continuing her questions in a rush. "And what's this place? Why did it call us witches? And a demigod? Do you guys really have powers? I mean, I know you have powers because I saw it, but *how* do you have powers? And since you all have them, do I have them, too?"

Her questions made my head spin, and I pressed

my fingers to my temples to stop the pounding. I tried to steady my breathing, but I had to gasp for air, like there wasn't enough oxygen left in it. Why did no one else notice that the cave was running out of oxygen? They all looked fine—even Kate, who stood up and walked over to us.

"You're Becca, right?" Kate asked, kneeling in front of her. "Nicole's sister?"

Becca nodded and crossed her arms. "Yeah," she said. "I am."

Kate tucked her hair behind her ears and managed a small smile. "Everything you saw here will take a while to explain," she said patiently. "But I promise I'll try my best to answer your questions once we're out of here and somewhere safe."

Danielle frowned and placed her hands on her hips. "That's a terrible idea," she said. "I know that immediate family members who aren't witches are allowed to know about us, but what she saw wasn't normal witchcraft. What if she freaks out and blabs about us to everyone? We should let Darius handle this."

"Danielle's right," Chris said. "We should bring Becca to Darius's house and have him talk to her."

"So that means you know how to get us out of here?" Becca asked.

"Sort of," Chris said. "We'll figure it out."

"We can't leave yet," Kate said. "First, Nicole needs to get the Book of Shadows." She looked at me, tilting her head towards the bookstand. "Do you need help getting over there?"

Judging from the concern in her eyes, I must have looked really weak. "I'm fine," I said, trying to force a smile and stand up. But the world spun, and I had to steady myself on my palms to keep from falling.

Before I could process what was happening, Blake picked me up and carried me over to the Book. I wrapped my arms around his neck and closed my eyes. His skin was so warm. I wanted to nestle into him and sleep forever.

"Nicole?" he whispered, his voice filled with concern. "We need you to lift the Book from the stand. After you do that, you can rest and leave it to me to get you out of here safely. Okay?"

I looked up at him, smiling at his warm eyes staring down at me. "Okay," I said, although I could barely get the word out. "Sounds good."

Footsteps sounded behind us, and Chris appeared next to the Book. He gave it a small tug, but it didn't budge. "It's stuck," he said.

Kate tried to lift it, too, but it still refused to move.

"The harpy must have been right that only you can get the Book," Chris said, looking at me. "You lift it and hand it to me, and I'll take charge of carrying it out of here, all right?"

"Put me down so I can get it," I told Blake, blinking a few times to make sure my eyes stayed open.

He eased me down, wrapping his arms around my waist when my feet hit the ground. "You okay?" he asked, his lips only millimeters from my ear. It felt nice to have him so close—warm. Like when we'd kissed at the bottom of the cliff, in the darkness where the others couldn't see.

Where *Danielle* couldn't see.

I shook away the memory and tried to focus. I had to give the Book of Shadows to Chris. Then Blake would pick me up again and I could rest in his arms while he got me out of the cave. It sounded so welcoming that I wanted to give in and close my eyes right now.

But first I had to get the Book.

Knowing that Blake wouldn't let me fall, I reached forward and wrapped my hands around the Book's edges. It was dusty—like it had been sitting in the cave for years. The dust stuck to my palms, making them dry and slippery. But somehow, I gathered the strength to lift it up.

I'd only lifted it an inch before Chris took it from my hands. The ground swayed beneath my feet, and Blake tightened his grip around me, lifting me back into his arms. I rested my head against his chest and listened to his heartbeat—slow and steady, like a lullaby.

He brushed a strand of hair off my face and tucked it behind my ear. "You did a great job," he whispered, trailing his finger down my cheek. My skin tingled at his touch. "If it weren't for you, I would have drowned in the ocean, and none of us would be here right now. You saved my life. And when you fell down that cliff..." He paused, and I heard his heart speed up. "I was terrified. I thought you were gone. All I could think about was—"

"Are we leaving or what?" Danielle's shrill voice filled the cave. "I've had enough of musty caves for the day. Can she walk?"

"Does it look like she can walk?" Chris's voice sounded muffled, like he'd gone somewhere else while Blake and I had been talking. Well, when Blake had been talking to me, since it took too much energy for me to add anything to the conversation. And what was he going to say before Danielle interrupted? All he could think about was ... what?

I wanted to ask, but I didn't have enough energy to speak.

"She used up more energy than she should have..." Kate trailed.

"She can borrow some of ours to heal herself," Chris suggested. "Like we did before."

"It's not that simple." Kate spoke so quietly that I had to strain to hear her. "It's different than what you did with me. And that was dangerous, too—if I had been conscious, I would have told you not to try it."

"How's it different?" Chris asked.

"We allowed Nicole to *channel* our energy to heal Kate so she didn't have to use as much of her own," Blake explained. I could feel the vibrations in his chest as he spoke. It felt nice against my cheek. "She transferred our energy into white energy without absorbing it into her own life force. Then she used that energy to heal Kate. If she had taken any for herself, she could have killed all of us in the process, since it's nearly impossible to break the connection once you start taking someone's energy. And after you do it once, that's it. You'll always need the energy of others to survive. There were enough of us to fend her off if she made a mistake and took our energy instead of conducting it, but even if she'd only taken a bit, it would have been too late. We would have turned her into a killer."

"So why did we give her our energy at all?" Chris asked. "Why didn't we let her try to heal Kate on her own?"

"Because she didn't have enough energy left, so she would have killed herself, and then Kate would have died, too," Danielle said. "And we need to all stay alive—even if it meant risking Nicole turning into an energy-sucking killer. Let's just be glad *that* didn't happen. Because once the Elders found out—"

"They wouldn't have found out," Blake interrupted. "We would have protected Nicole. No matter what."

"It's irrelevant, because none of us are killers," Kate said. "We're all fine."

Ice ran through my veins, and I stayed as still as possible, glad that my eyes were closed and no one could see the guilt I was feeling. Because while it was different than what they were discussing, I was exactly what they feared. A killer.

I'd killed the harpy just by touching it.

I knew now more than ever—no one could know about what I'd done. Because I doubted I wanted to know firsthand what the punishment would be if the Elders found out.

Keeping it secret was the only way to ensure I stayed safe.

"There has to be something we can do for her now," Chris said. "Look at her. She can't even walk."

"As long as she doesn't use up any more energy, she'll probably just need rest," Kate said. "But we have to take her to Darius. He'll know what to do for her."

I wanted to help them get out of here. How were they going to get out without me?

But just the thought of opening my eyes was exhausting, and I finally gave in and let sleep claim me, unable to stay awake for any longer.

CHAPTER THIRTY-NINE

The first thing I felt when I woke up was heat on my face. The sun.

Which would have been normal, except my bedroom didn't have any windows facing east, so the sunlight didn't enter in the morning.

The lack of morning light made me miss my room in Georgia.

Maybe I *was* still in my room in Georgia. Maybe all of that witch stuff was a dream, and I would open my eyes and be back in my old house, getting ready to start school again after winter break. Everything that had happened recently was certainly strange enough to have been a dream—a very strange, vivid dream.

But my throat was so dry, as if I hadn't had water

in days. I swallowed, and it felt like a hundred tiny knives jabbing the back of my throat. My tongue had swelled up and felt like sandpaper. I needed water. But first I needed enough energy to stand up and get it. And right now, I could barely manage to roll over.

"Nicole?" a quiet voice asked. "Are you awake?"

Footsteps sounded nearby, getting closer until whoever it was placed something on the nightstand—a glass, judging from the clink as it hit the surface. "If you're up, there's ice water for you on the table," she continued. "It might help you get some energy back."

I pictured what the water must look like—the cool glass covered with condensation—and my throat burned with the thought. Crust coated my eyes, and I pried them open, greeted by the light of the sun shining through a window. The window was unfamiliar—chestnut panels with thin green drapes.

"You're up!" the voice exclaimed. I turned my head and saw Kate.

The hope that my life in Kinsley had been a crazy dream disappeared. Everything was real—up to the ugly bird creature who'd captured my sister and tried to kill us in a cave that we'd entered through a shimmering rock-portal in the woods.

"Where am I?" I asked, the words scratchy in my throat. Remembering the water next to the bed, I reached for it and downed it in a few gulps.

"We're at my house." Kate dragged over a wooden chair and placed it next to the bed, sitting down to face me. "You passed out after giving the Book of Shadows to Chris. None of us had enough energy to go back the way we'd entered, so we tested our luck with the other shimmery portal in the chamber. It led us to the playground at the Hemlock Center. The place was trashed—like a gang war had broken out there or something." She stopped to take a breath, and continued, "We called Darius, and he picked us up and brought us back to my car. You almost depleted your energy in the cave, but Darius said you needed time to naturally replenish it and you would be okay. So I brought you back here so you could sleep it off."

I pushed myself up and leaned against the bedpost. "I feel better than what I last remember in the cave," I said. "But what about Becca? Is she back, too? She must be freaking out. What did you all tell her?"

"Darius made her forget everything." Kate's voice was flat. "He brought her back to your house. He also made your parents think you had called to tell them you were sleeping at my house, and then he made them forget that he had been there at all."

"He can do that?" I blinked a few times, shocked.

"Yes," she said. "All of the Elders can. But they only tamper with memory if it's an emergency."

It sounded like a questionable practice, but I had other concerns right now. "How long have I been sleeping?" I asked.

"About thirteen or fourteen hours," she said. "But you're feeling better, right?"

"Not the greatest, but I'll survive." I brought my legs to my chest and wrapped my arms around them. "I feel more like I stayed up all night partying as opposed to healing three people—including myself—who were close to death, and staking a monster with a stalagmite."

Kate pushed her hair behind her ears and laughed. "The others will want to know that you're okay," she said, serious again. "I'll call them in a minute—do you want some more water?"

"Yes." I nodded and licked my lips. My throat and tongue were still so dry that it felt like I could drink a bathtub full of water if she placed one in front of me. "Thanks."

She walked out the door and gently shut it behind her, leaving me to reflect over everything that had happened. At least Darius had made Becca forget everything so I wouldn't have to get her involved in all of this. But that creature had managed to get its hands on her, and there was no reason to believe that anything else that escaped Kerberos would be less merciful towards humans—especially the humans closest to their enemies.

I lowered my head to balance it on my knees. How was I supposed to be ready for this? The others had known about their powers for all of their lives. I'd just learned about mine a week and a half ago. Now I was expected to fight in an age-old battle with creatures that had far more experience than I could ever hope for. If the prophecy was right, and this is what I was supposed to do, then fate had a funny way of dealing with things. Because people are supposed to *train* for battle before entering it.

Apparently I wasn't going to get that opportunity.

The door opened again, and I lifted my head, forcing

a smile when I met Kate's eyes. She carried another glass of water—this one bigger than the first. I grabbed it and gulped it down.

"Feeling better?" she asked.

"Yes," I said, placing the empty glass on the nightstand. "The water helped a lot. Thanks."

"No problem." She sat on the end of the bed and leaned against the wall, her legs straight in front of her so her feet hung over the edge. "I called Darius," she said. "He said to come over to his house if you were feeling up to it. He'll call the others, too. He wants to talk with us about the Book of Shadows. It was ... well, he'll explain when we get there."

"Was there something wrong with the Book?" I asked.

"Darius just wants us all together to figure out what to do next," she said. "From what the harpy told us, we're going to have bigger challenges ahead than a treasure hunt for the Book of Shadows."

"What did the stuff that the harpy said even mean?" I asked, trying to recall the specifics. "Something about a demigod and a typhon. Isn't that some kind of giant wave?"

Kate looked down at the bed, chewing her bottom lip. "We should wait to get to Darius's so he can explain. But first, you need to eat. My family was hungry and didn't want to wake us before they went to brunch, so we can just have breakfast here."

My stomach growled, and I stretched my arms, a rush of energy returning to my system. "I'm ready," I said. "We'll have breakfast, and then we'll head out."

"Okay." She studied me and pushed herself off the bed. "Remember to keep an open mind about what Darius is going to say. It might sound strange ..." She paused and looked down at her hands. "Well, I'll let you decide for yourself. Come on."

CHAPTER FORTY

The front door to Darius's house was unlocked, and I followed Kate into the great room. Darius sat in a red armchair, and Chris, Blake, and Danielle were on the matching couch. They watched me with relieved looks on their faces—even Danielle's.

Chris jumped out of his seat before I had a chance to say hi. "Nicole!" he said, motioning me to join them. "Take my seat. I can sit on the floor."

"Thanks." I walked over to the couch, trying not to look at Blake as I sat down. His kissing me in the cave had changed everything, but I had no idea what it meant for us—if it meant anything to him at all. Because as far as I was aware, he still hadn't broken up with Danielle. I needed to talk to him, without everyone else listening. But for now, I scooted as close to the side of the couch as possible, balancing my elbow on the armrest and trying not to look at him.

Chris sat cross-legged in front of the coffee table, the Book of Shadows placed on top of it. The leather cover was aged and ancient, and the yellowed paper wasn't all the same length, making it look like one of the old novels in my grandfather's library. However, the Book was bigger than a novel—it was closer to the size of a dictionary.

Blake's eyes met mine, and I sucked in a breath at the intensity of his gaze. "I'm glad you're doing better," he said. "We were all worried about you back in the cave. I thought ... well, I'm just glad that you're okay."

My skin tingled at the depth of concern in his voice. I would definitely have to figure out how to talk with him—alone—later. But for now I managed a small smile and turned back to Darius, who studied me with equal worry.

"Yes, we're all glad you're okay," Darius said.

I crossed my legs away from Blake and looked at the Book. "So, what's in the Book?" I asked, resisting the urge to reach forward and open it myself.

"Before we get to that, we need to talk about what the harpy said to you." Darius looked at Danielle and nodded once. "What were her exact words again?"

"I don't remember her *exact* words," Danielle said. "But she said that Typhon was rising, and that he needed to 'return to his true form.' And ..." She narrowed her eyes at me. "She called Nicole a demigod."

"Aren't we all demigods?" I asked. "We're descended from the Greek gods."

"We're *witches*," Danielle clarified. "The diluted god blood in our veins enables us to access energy to perform magic. But each generation gets weaker if the god blood is mixed with human blood, until the ability to do magic disappears completely. If we keep our blood pure, the magic we pass down will stay strong. That's why we're encouraged to marry other witches and not spend much time with humans. But a *demigod* is the direct offspring of a god and a mortal. Half god, half human. It's different."

"So if I'm a demigod, then one of my parents would have to be ..." I trailed off, unable to say it out loud.

"One of your parents would have to be a god," Blake finished my thought. "And you've never met your bio-dad, so it's possible."

"So you're saying my bio-dad's a *god*?" I looked at Darius for confirmation. He stared back at me, his eyes serious. "That's ridiculous." I laughed. "I didn't develop my powers, or even *know* about them, until I got here. If I were a demigod—" I paused, shaking my head at the word. "I would have realized it earlier. Right?"

"The Head Elders block the powers of a demigod until they're ready to use them, or until their powers strengthen enough to overcome the spell," Darius said, his gaze unwavering. "To keep the young demigods safe, the Head Elders don't tell anyone outside of their inner circle about who they are. The birth of a demigod is uncommon nowadays, since the gods don't come to

Earth as often, but it happens. Blocking their powers lowers the risk of a young demigod losing control and seriously injuring people without meaning to. Let's go back to how you accidentally blew up that glass the other day." He paused, and I pictured the moment. "Now imagine a two-year-old demigod having a temper tantrum. It's safer for you to not know about your powers until you're mature enough to control them."

"So let's say the harpy was right and I *am* a demigod," I said. "That would mean you must have some idea who my father is. Right?"

Darius nodded, a smile creeping up on his lips. "I've been thinking about that," he said. "You're a fantastic tennis player, which means you have good aim. Your friends tell me that you get intuitions about things, and that those intuitions are usually right. Your special ability is healing. I looked up your mother on the Internet because I was curious to see which god might have been attracted to her, and found that she's a singer and an artist. Which would likely bring her attention from ..." He looked around and waited for one of the others to complete the sentence, like we were in class instead of talking in his living room.

"Apollo," Kate finished, her mouth wide open. "You're the daughter of Apollo."

I thought about the little bit of Greek mythology I'd learned during the past few days. "The god of the sun?" I asked.

"Among many other things." Kate leaned forward and explained, "Apollo's mainly the god of healing, archery, music, the arts, and prophecy."

"Healing makes sense," I said, sitting back in the couch. "Archery could explain why I have good aim." I flashed back to the fight with the hound and how easy it had been for me to shoot the monkey bar through its heart. "I've always liked music. I've taught myself a bit of guitar, but I've never taken a lesson."

"You should try," Chris said. "Maybe you'll be the next Hendrix." He played a few notes on air-guitar, breaking some of the tension in the room and making everyone laugh.

"Okay," I agreed. "But is there any way to prove this? I'm going to have a tough time believing it without any proof."

Darius shook his head. "It's only a theory. We may or may not get proof in the future, but as of now, everything is pointing in the direction of you being a demigod."

"So I'm a demigod." It sounded ridiculous when said aloud. "Let's say that you're right. Is there some kind of rule that gods can't visit their kids? Because I've never met my bio-dad. It would've been nice to have him in my life growing up, and he's immortal, so he must have had time. Does he even care that he has a kid?"

"The gods are busy," Darius said with a sigh. "It's not that they don't care—"

"It's common for the gods to ignore their children," Danielle interrupted. "The only way for a demigod to get a god's attention is to do something spectacular, like Perseus who slayed Medusa or Hercules who killed some of the most dangerous monsters out there. I doubt that grabbing a book and killing a random harpy is going to cut it."

I waited for Darius to say she was wrong, but he remained silent.

"Is that true?" I finally asked. "The gods ignore their kids?"

"He's not ignoring you," Darius said gently. "I'm sure he's just very busy. And now there's a war going on. Perhaps he'll speak with you sometime in the future."

The smug smile remained on Danielle's face. "Doubtful," she said. "Anyway, what's going on with the Book of Shadows? Any change since last night?"

Darius gave me a half-hearted smile and looked back at the Book. "Not that I know of," he said. "But I haven't looked at it again since you first brought it over. Perhaps it will change if Nicole gives it a try. Since she was the only one who could lift it off the podium, maybe she's the only one who can access what's inside."

"What do you mean by that?" I asked.

Darius motioned towards the Book. "Look for yourself."

I lowered myself in front of the coffee table, balancing my knees on the floor and leaning over the Book. While the plain leather cover resembled something from hundreds of years ago, there wasn't a scratch on it. It was like it had been transported through time, never touched by human hands.

I reached for it and was surprised by how warm it was—like it was alive. The cover opened easily, and I held my breath in anticipation of what I was about to see.

A blank page stared back at me. I flipped through a few more pages, and they were all the same.

"There's nothing in here." I looked up at Darius, waiting for an explanation.

He sat back in his chair and focused on the Book. "Which means nothing's changed."

"So this Book of Shadows is supposed to help us save the world, and it's empty," Chris said. "How's that helpful?"

"The gods must have a plan," Kate said. "Otherwise, why would the prophecy lead us to the Book?"

Darius placed his hands in his lap, looking around at all of us. "All will be revealed in time," he said. "Leave the Book of Shadows with me. If there are any changes, you five will be the first to know."

"So we just go home?" Danielle asked.

"Yes." Darius nodded. "I want Blake to study the book he received in his clue and start making those weapons. Judging from the trials you five just faced, they will be necessary. The rest of you should do whatever you can to help him. I'm going to devise a special training program so you all can learn to use your new powers to the best of your abilities. I need a few days to talk with the Head Elders and figure out exactly what's going on here, and in the meantime, I put protection spells around the school and your houses to stop monsters from getting inside."

"That creature got to Becca so easily," I said. "Even with the protection spell up, it could have just waited for her to leave the house and gotten her then. How are we supposed to stop them?"

"By getting to them first," Darius said, completely serious.

My head spun with a million thoughts a second. The Book that was supposed to help us save the world was empty. The portal to Kerberos had weakened enough that monsters were escaping. And then there was the other thing the harpy had said...

"What's a typhon?" I asked, hoping I got the name correct. "The harpy said something about a typhon. What does that mean?"

"You mean *who*," Kate said, her expression grim. "Typhon is one of the most dangerous monsters out there. If he gets loose ..." She paused to take a breath. "I don't see how we can beat him. But the harpy told us that Typhon had to 'return to his true form.' And his true form is—"

"As tall as a mountain," Blake interrupted, holding his hands high in the air. "With a hundred heads, vipers for legs, fire in his eyes ... well, that's an exaggeration to scare people, but basically, we don't want to have to fight him. We won't stand a chance."

"Maybe we won't *have* to fight him," Chris said. "We just have to kill him before he reaches his true form."

"And where's his true form?" I asked.

"Zeus struck him down with lightning a long time ago and trapped him under Mount Etna, which is in Sicily, Italy," Kate replied, her eyes lighting up at the chance to share her knowledge. "The Titans wanted to free Typhon in the Second Rebellion, since he's the deadliest monster out there, but Zeus forced them into Kerberos before they could reach him. Then Zeus split Typhon's soul from his body and put his soul in Kerberos, while keeping his body under the mountain. It makes it twice as hard for him to escape." She looked down at her fingernails and shrugged. "I wish you all had more time to talk with the harpy before killing her. Maybe she could have given us more information…"

"Or she would have killed us first," Blake interrupted. "We did the right thing by stopping her when we did."

"Yes." Darius nodded. "What you did was very brave. But do me a favor and don't tell anyone yet. There's no need to cause a panic before we know exactly what's going on. I'll tell the others in homeroom on a need to know basis once we have more information. Until then, stay quiet about it."

"But the others can help us fight." Chris leaned forward and smacked his fist into his palm. "Shouldn't we start training as soon as possible?"

"We can only start official training when we know what we're up against," Darius said. "Hopefully it won't take too long to figure it out and develop a strategy. But for now, stay focused on making those weapons and practicing your powers."

"It makes sense to me," Kate agreed. "What else can we do to help?"

"Go home and act like nothing's changed," he instructed. "Work on improving your skills." He faced me, his expression serious. "And Nicole—I'm sure Kate has already told you that I've wiped your sister's memory of everything that happened. We couldn't risk her telling others what she saw—especially humans."

I remembered what Becca had looked like with her wrists and ankles tied to the chair, helpless to protect herself. I was just glad that she was okay. "It's for the best," I told Darius. "Becca isn't good at keeping secrets."

"Now, I have to leave to meet with the Head Elders in DC so we can discuss the details of what's going on." Darius leaned forward and closed the Book. "And it's time for you to all go home and get some rest so you're ready for school in the morning. Until I get back, don't go anywhere except for school and your houses—the places where the protection spells are up. As I will be out of town, there will be a substitute in for me. I'm sure you know to pretend that our homeroom is completely normal."

Normal. I rolled my eyes. My life was anything *but* normal nowadays.

We said goodnight, and everyone was silent as they stood up—probably taking in everything we'd discussed. The new information was still spinning in my mind, too.

"Why don't you let me take you home?" Blake asked me as I put on my coat. He watched me closely, and I flashed back to when he kissed me in the cave, my heart beating faster at the memory. "I'm meeting my family for a late lunch, and the restaurant is only a block from your house."

I looked at Kate to see what she thought, since she

was the one who had driven me here. She lowered her eyes, as if telling me to do whatever I wanted, and I turned back to Blake. "Okay." I tried to keep my voice from wavering. "I guess that makes sense."

Danielle walked over to us, swinging her keys. "I'll see you tonight," she said to Blake. Her voice was firm and controlled, like she was trying to hold back anger but not doing a good job. She leaned forward and kissed him, and even though he was about as responsive as a wooden board, my blood boiled just the same. "Call me when you get home."

"Will do," he said, and then he looked back at me with guilt in his eyes. "You ready?"

A lump formed in my throat, and I swallowed to make it go away. "Yeah," I said. "Thanks for offering to drive."

I acted as normal as possible while saying bye to Kate and thanking her for taking care of me while I recovered. The determination in her eyes let me know that there was no way I was escaping her giving me the third degree later about what was going on between Blake and me. And I was terrible at lying, so I would have to tell her. At least I trusted that she would keep it secret.

For now, Blake and I walked towards his Range Rover in silence. He opened the door for me, and I smiled in thanks, wondering as he walked around to the driver's side if he was going to bring up our kiss in the cave. He most likely would.

Then I would have to tell him that as long as he stayed with Danielle, nothing like that could ever happen between us again.

CHAPTER FORTY-ONE

Blake barely looked at me as he pulled out of the driveway, and I fidgeted in my seat, glancing out the window. It seemed like it was going to be up to me to start this conversation.

"What was 'all you could think about?'" I finally asked.

He looked at me, his eyebrows furrowed.

"You started to say that in the cave, but Danielle interrupted you before you could tell me," I explained.

"All I could think about..." He focused on the road as he repeated the words. "When the harpy pushed you off the cliff, all I could think about was how much it would kill me if you didn't survive the fall." He tightened his grip around the steering wheel, and continued, "I don't know how to explain it, but I've felt connected to you since I saw you walk into homeroom on your first day. It's unlike anything I've ever felt for Danielle. Do you have the same thing? Or am I going crazy?" He glanced at me for the first time since getting in the car, the intensity in his eyes sending a wave of heat through my body.

"I do feel the same way," I said. "But what happened in the cave ... it can't happen again." I paused, my voice catching in my throat. "Because even if you break up with Danielle, she's still part of our group. The five of us are bound together whether we want to be or not. If you and me are together, what if Danielle gets so angry when she finds out that she refuses to work with us? Without her, we might not be able to fight like we need to. It would put not just us, but our families, in danger. And after what that harpy did to Becca, I can't risk that happening."

Saying it made me feel empty inside. But I was doing the right thing.

So why didn't it feel like it?

"We can figure it out," he said, his knuckles white as he gripped the wheel. "We could be together in secret."

"And have to lie to everyone?" I asked. "And constantly feel like we're doing something wrong? I can't do that."

"It wouldn't be like that forever," he said. "Don't say no yet. Take some time to think about it."

"I can't," I said. "Especially not while you're still with Danielle."

"My decision hasn't changed," he said. "I haven't had time to talk to Danielle yet to let her know that it's over between us, but I plan on doing it soon. I promise."

We were both silent for a few seconds, and just when I was about to make some filler comment about the weather, he added, "I should have known you were a demigod from the start. I can't believe I didn't realize it sooner."

"Even Darius didn't know," I said. "Why would *you* have been able to realize it if he couldn't?"

"Never mind." He shook his head. "Forget I said anything."

"You can't do that."

He raised an eyebrow. "Can't do what?"

"Start saying something and stop. If you don't want to say anything, then don't start. It's like the 'not telling someone you have a secret if you don't plan on sharing it' rule."

He laughed, his eyes brightening. "There's a rule for that?"

"Yes." I smiled and crossed my arms over my chest. "You started to say that you should have realized I was a demigod—despite the fact that even Darius doesn't have the power to know that. Now you *have* to tell me what you were going to say. If you don't, it'll drive me crazy."

"Maybe I *want* to drive you crazy." He smirked.

Heat rose to my cheeks, and for a few seconds, I was speechless. "Come on," I finally said. "Spill."

"I was referring to how your powers are so strong,"

he said. "I was the only one who saw when you defeated the hound at the playground. I should have thought about it and fit the pieces together. If Kate had been with you, I guarantee it would have crossed her mind."

"Maybe." I shrugged. "Or maybe not. But don't act like it was all me—the two of us defeated the hound *together*. And you did an amazing job with the harpy. We couldn't have killed her without you."

"I guess you're right," he said. "We do make a great team."

"But even with our new powers, I don't know how we're going to do this," I said. "We're up against every evil creature in existence that sided with Typhon and the Titans in the Second Rebellion."

"And maybe even Typhon and the Titans themselves," he added, his lips straightening into a grim line.

"Darius and the Head Elders better have an amazing plan."

"They'll come up with something," he said. "And remember—we have the Olympian gods on our side. If it comes to it, they'll fight with us. They'll have to."

I hoped more than anything that he was right.

We chatted for the rest of the ride, and it didn't take long to reach my house. He pulled into my driveway and came to a stop.

I took my seatbelt off and faced him, not wanting to leave yet. "Thanks for taking me home," I said, pushing my hair behind my ears. Even though I'd just told him that nothing could happen between us, my heart pounded harder than ever, and I watched him in expectation, wondering what he would do.

If he kissed me again, I wouldn't be able to resist.

"Like I said, your house is only a block away from where I'm going." His formal tone surprised me, and he sat so straight and rigid. It was like there was a wall between us. Which I should have been grateful for—since it was what I'd ask for—but it disappointed me anyway. "I'll see you in school tomorrow."

"Right." I hopped out of the car, although I didn't close the door. "And thanks for everything you did in the cave. If you hadn't come up with the idea of letting me channel your energy, I wouldn't have been able to heal Kate."

"It wasn't too hard to think of," he said simply. "It's just something that no one ever talks about because of the risks. But you were going to try healing her even though you didn't have enough energy left to do it, and I couldn't let you die. I would never be able to forgive myself if that had happened."

With those words, the energy between us grew stronger, like a string pulling me towards him. I wanted to take back everything I'd said earlier, about how we couldn't be together.

But if Blake knew what I did to the harpy—using black energy to kill it with a single touch—would he still feel the same way about me? Or would he be scared?

I couldn't be sure.

So as hard as it was, I said goodnight and headed inside, not looking back as he drove away.

CHAPTER FORTY-TWO

When I got inside, I found my mom in her studio finishing up the painting I'd seen earlier that week. She didn't question it when I told her I was going to take a nap. She probably assumed Kate and I had stayed up all night talking, like I usually did when I slept over my friends' houses back in Georgia.

I peeked inside Becca's room on the way to mine. She sat at her computer, either doing homework or messaging her friends—probably the latter. She'd pulled her hair back into a messy bun, and she wore a red sweatshirt from her middle school back in Georgia. Dark circles rimmed her normally bright eyes. I'd never seen her so exhausted. Even though Darius had wiped her memory, could she possibly still remember anything from yesterday?

She must have heard me approach, because she rotated her chair and smirked. "Did you have fun this weekend?" she asked, waggling her eyebrows. "Especially on Friday night, in particular?"

I almost asked her what had happened on Friday night, but then I remembered—that was the night I'd sneaked out with Blake. So much had happened since then that it didn't feel like it had only been two days ago.

And judging by how relaxed Becca was being about it, I knew Darius's mind trick had worked. Becca didn't remember the harpy kidnapping her, or anything that had happened in the cave. She was safe. I had to resist the urge to run up to her and give her a big hug. However, Darius had said to act like everything was normal, and that definitely wouldn't be a normal thing for me to do.

"Yeah, tons." I rolled my eyes, forcing sarcasm into my tone. "Thanks for asking. I owe you one for covering for me."

"How about you tell me who it was you met up with, and we'll call it even?"

"It doesn't matter who it was," I mumbled. "Because nothing can happen between me and him. It was a one-time thing."

"So it *was* a guy!" She smiled in victory. Then the sound of a message dinged on her computer, and she read it, typing up a response. Whoever she was talking to had distracted her for now.

Glad that our conversation seemed to be over, I

headed back to my room and collapsed onto my bed. But the sun shining through the window kept me awake, and eventually I forced myself back up so I could close the blinds.

A small, wooden box sitting outside my window made me freeze in place. That definitely hadn't been there yesterday. I pried the window open and pulled the box inside. It fit in the palm of my hand, and the golden latch easily popped open.

Inside sat a delicate golden charm in the shape of a sun, strung through a matching chain. It reminded me of the pendant that Blake had made for me in ceramics, except the smoothness of this one was much finer and better crafted.

I closed the window, placed the box on my bed, and took out the necklace. The sun charm hummed against my skin, glowing with a light of its own. Like magic.

I rotated it in my palm, stopping when I saw an engraving on the back—an elegant "A" carved into the metal. I traced my fingers over the letter, allowing its meaning to sink in.

Maybe Darius's idea of Apollo being my father wasn't so far-fetched after all.

ELEMENTALS

THE BLOOD OF THE HYDRA

Book two in the Elementals series

COMING APRIL 2016

Read on for a sneak peak!

CHAPTER ONE

I held steady onto my bow, the arrow pointed straight at the bull's-eye. As always, my mind knew exactly what to do—the stance I should take, how to hold the weapon, and how to balance my weight. I drew the bowstring back, aimed, and let the arrow soar.

It missed the target, instead embedding itself in the wall.

"Chris!" I yelled, dropping the bow to my side and spinning around. Sure enough, Chris stood behind me, his hands raised as if to protect himself from flying arrows. "Stop using your powers on me during practice. That would have been a perfect shot."

He smirked, and a breeze blew past my face. The next thing I knew, an arrow from my quiver floated up and propelled itself straight into the bulls-eye. *"There's a perfect shot,"* he said, pumping his fist up in victory.

"We're supposed to be practicing using weapons *without* our powers right now," I reminded him. "Just because Darius had to go upstairs to take a call doesn't mean we can do whatever we want." I took out another arrow, balanced it on the bow again, and released.

It joined the other straight on the bulls-eye.

I used to think I was a natural at tennis. But that was nothing compared to how quickly I'd picked up on archery. Which, according to Kate, made sense, since Apollo was my father. One of his talents was said to be archery.

Although of course, I'd learned this all from what Kate had told me, since I'd never actually met my father.

"Want to try?" I asked Chris, holding the bow out to him in challenge. "*Without* using your power?"

"You know I can't use that." He walked over to the selection of weapons laid out on the counter and picked up a knife, smiling as he examined it. "But this, I've been practicing with. Check it out."

He geared up and threw the knife towards the target.

It landed further away than my first arrow.

"I'm getting better," he said sheepishly. "When I first started, it kept bouncing off the wall and onto the floor." He used his power to lift another knife from the counter and shoot it at the target. This time, it landed straight in the center. "It's so much easier that way," he said.

"Until you use your powers so much that you run out of energy," I said. "You know what Darius told us. We can train and learn how to use weapons ourselves. We have to save our energy to use our powers when we really need them."

"I know, I know." Chris sighed, exasperated, and pushed his hair out of his eyes. I knew why he was frustrated—we'd been practicing every day after school since our fight with the harpy, but Chris hadn't picked up on using weapons as fast as the rest of us.

"You just need to practice," I said. "Your powers help you more with using weapons than any of the rest of ours do, but if you keep using them as a crutch, you're never going to get better."

He raised his hands up again, and both arrows and knives floated back to us. The arrows settled themselves back inside my quiver, and the knives came straight back to his hands.

"Our powers do come in handy, though," he said with a wink. "Less clean up time."

"Isn't this supposed to be no power hour?" Blake asked, strolling over to join us. In his all-black training outfit, he looked like he had years of experience on Chris, who wore sweats and a t-shirt. And his warm eyes were focused straight on me, which as always, took my breath away.

But even though he'd broken up with Danielle soon after our fight with the harpy, he was still off-limits. Because the five of us—me, Blake, Danielle, Chris, and Kate—were a team. We had to learn to work together.

And dating Danielle's boyfriend right after Blake had broken up with her would put a huge rift in that team.

I picked up another arrow, strung it in the bow, and released it straight into the bulls-eye.

"No powers." I glanced at Blake over my shoulder and smiled. "That was all natural talent."

"Except I'm pretty sure I just saw some arrows and knives flying—*towards* both of you," he said. "And as far as I'm aware, the wall doesn't have much of an aim."

"Guilty as charged," Chris said, holding both knives in the air. With his bright eyes and boyish grin, he looked more like he was preparing for a cooking challenge than for battling ancient mythological monsters.

"Since you're over here breaking the rules, I figured I would join," Blake said, pulling his lighter out of his pocket. "Have you ever shot a flaming arrow?"

"No." I smiled at where this was going. "But I think now would be a great time to try."

"I thought you might say that." He walked closer until he was standing only a foot away from me, his eyes not leaving mine the entire time. I couldn't move, couldn't breathe—all I could do was focus on him. He flicked on the lighter, picked up an arrow, and dipped it into the flame.

I worried that the flame might go out—after all, I doubted the arrows were meant to be lit on fire—but it held strong. Blake was getting better with using his power every day.

"Here." He held the flaming arrow out to me. "Try it

now."

I reached for it, and my fingers brushed against his. Heat traveled up my arms and to my cheeks, and I moved my gaze away from his to focus on the target, hoping he hadn't noticed the affect he had on me.

I steadied my stance, lifted the bow to eye-level, and strung the arrow as usual. But the flame danced before my eyes, reminding me that this was anything *but* normal. This was magic. I pulled back on the bowstring, feeling Blake's eyes on me, and reminded myself to focus despite the distraction of the fire. I aimed and released, sending the arrow straight to the target. It wasn't a bulls-eye, but it was close.

A few seconds passed, and the flames eventually died out.

"Let's try again," Blake said, taking a few steps back. "How far away is that target?"

"About sixty feet," I answered.

"Which is much farther than I can aim with my fireballs," he said. "My aim's good for about ten to twenty feet, and that's it. And I'm nowhere near as good with shooting weapons as you are. We might not always be right next to each other in a fight, but we can still work together. Are you ready?"

"For what?"

He flicked the lighter on again, balancing another ball of fire in his hand. "String the bow, and I'll show you."

I did as he said, the arrow pointed straight to the target. "Now what?" I asked.

"Don't flinch."

He threw the fireball at the tip of the arrow, which burst into flame, and caused me to jump. "Hey!" I yelled at him. "You could have warned me."

"I did." He laughed. "I told you not to flinch."

"Yeah, yeah." I corrected my stance and pulled back on the bowstring, sending the arrow straight towards the bulls-eye.

"Again," Blake instructed, and I drew another arrow. This time, I knew to expect the flame. Once the arrow was ablaze, I released it to the target, and grabbed another. It was like my body was working on super speed, and the rush was unlike anything I'd ever experienced. I didn't want to stop. So we kept going— Blake lighting up the arrow and me shooting—until all of the arrows were gone from the quiver and embedded in the target.

"Wow," I said, catching my breath as I admired the arrows still on fire.

The blaze grew taller, and then it exploded, engulfing the target completely. Before I knew what was happening, a stream of water flew towards the target, extinguishing the fire.

"What do you think you're doing?" Danielle's voice echoed through the practice chamber. "Trying to burn down our training center?"

"We were practicing a new technique," I said. "We must have gotten carried away."

"You could say that." Danielle coughed, fanning the smoke out of her face. A breeze blew through the air— courtesy of Chris—who sent the smoke out of the window near the ceiling of the basement.

"Think of it this way," Blake said. "If that had been a monster's head, it would be dead by now."

Kate burst in from the shooting room, gun in hand. Strength-wise, she was the weakest of the five of us, so a gun had quickly become her weapon of choice. It had taken her a while to warm up to using such an intense weapon, but now she held onto it so naturally that it could have been an extra appendage.

"I smelled smoke," she said, her mouth dropping open when she saw the destroyed target. "What happened in here?"

We caught her up on what we'd done, Blake and I alternating on telling different parts of the story.

"There's no water in here," Kate said once we were finished, turning to Danielle. "If there's no water, how did you put out the fire?"

"There's water in the air," Danielle said, as if it should be obvious. "I condensed it into liquid and used it to put out the fire." She looked over at Blake and smiled, although it seemed strained. "You aren't the only ones who have been practicing."

"Except this is supposed to be no power hour," Kate said, holding up her gun. "Remember what happened with the harpy? We used all our energy killing it. We were lucky that there was that portal from the cave to the playground, but what if that hadn't been there? We would have been stuck in that cave for who knows how long. We need to get better as using weapons, so we only use our powers when we absolutely need them."

"They were doing it first." Danielle huffed. "When I

saw the target explode, I figured I would actually do something useful by putting out the fire."

"And I wasn't using my power," I said. "I was practicing archery."

"You weren't using your power because your power can't help you defend yourself," Danielle said.

"Whoa there," Blake said, holding his arms out. "No need to get nasty."

"I was just saying it like it is." Danielle shrugged, her eyes flashing with hurt. "And you have no right to tell me what to do. You lost that privilege when you dumped me."

I looked back and forth between the two of them, reminded again about why Blake and I couldn't be together. Danielle clearly wasn't over him. There was also so much I wanted to say, but I kept my mouth shut. Because Danielle had no idea about what I could really do. She and the others only knew about my power to heal. (Which I actually think is quite useful in battle, seeing as it's the power that can end up saving us all.) None of them knew about the other side of my power—the ability to kill with a touch. It was how I'd killed the harpy. I'd called on black energy, touched the harpy, and sent the energy into its body, which killed it instantly.

They all thought that the harpy had died because I'd staked it with a stalagmite. And they could never know the truth. Because using black energy ... it was illegal. If anyone found out about what I could do, I could have my powers stripped. Or worse.

I shivered at the thought, and wrapped my arms

around myself. I didn't want to know what the Head Elders might do to me if they found out about the true extent of my abilities. Which was why I had to keep them secret from everyone—even from the other Elementals.

"We should clean up," I said, changing the subject. "And I guess we'll be needing a new target. That one is pretty ..."

"Cooked?" Blake smirked, finishing my sentence. "Fried?"

"Yeah." I laughed. "Exactly."

"I'll help you clean up, but I won't be the one telling Darius," Kate said. "That's up to one of you."

We didn't have time to debate who would be telling him that we'd destroyed yet *another* piece of training equipment, because he came running into the practice room, swinging the door open with so much force that it banged against the wall. His eyes were wide, his hair mussed up, and his glasses crooked on the tip of his nose.

"Gather your weapons and meet me at my van." He looked at each of us, unfazed by the charred target. "A monster's been spotted at the Hemlock Center."

* * *

If you enjoyed this book, please remember to leave a review at your favorite retailer. Positive reviews are the best way to thank an author for writing a book you loved.

ACKNOWLEDGEMENTS

I wrote Elementals when I was a senior in college, and it's come a long way since then. I'm so happy to finally be able to share it with you!

First of all, a big thanks to Anne Madow, Christine Witthohn, and Brent Taylor, who helped me through multiple rounds of edits with this book.

My writing professors, Twila Papay and Phillip Deaver—thank you for approving my independent study in college, as this was the book that resulted from that.

My publicists, Danielle Barclay and Cameron Yeager—thank you so much for EVERYTHING you do! An amazing team is necessary for an author, and I'm so happy to be able to work with both of you.

Elise Kova—thank you for your amazing marketing advice, and for being such an incredible author friend! Your success with Air Awakens inspired me to publish

Elementals. I'm so happy to be on this journey together!

Kim Killion, my cover designer, and her assistant Megan Jordan—the cover is AMAZING! The moment I saw it, I was in awe. It's so perfect for the book, and I can't wait to see the covers for the rest of the series!

My brother, Steven Madow—you've always said that Elementals is your favorite book of mine. Thank you for your constant enthusiasm and for helping me believe that this book deserved to be published.

My dad, Richard Madow—thank you for encouraging and supporting my goal to publish Elementals, and for believing in my goal to be a hybrid author. And thank you for helping me edit the back cover blurb.

My mom, Anne Madow—thank you for helping me with all the detail-oriented tasks so that I can focus on writing more books!

And, of course, my Street Team, for being the best fans EVER!

ABOUT THE AUTHOR

Michelle Madow grew up in Baltimore, graduated Rollins College in Orlando, and now lives in Boca Raton, Florida. She wrote her first book in her junior year of college, and has been writing novels since. Some of her favorite things are: reading, pizza, traveling, shopping, time travel, Broadway musicals, and spending time with friends and family. Michelle has toured across America to promote her books and to encourage high school students to embrace reading and writing. Someday, she hopes to travel the world for a year on a cruise ship.

Follow her on:
Facebook:/MichelleMadow
Twitter/Instagram: @MichelleMadow
Snapchat: MichLMadow

Visit Michelle online at www.michellemadow.com.

To get exclusive content and instant updates on Michelle's new books, visit her website and subscribe to her newsletter!

CPSIA information can be obtained
at www.ICGtesting.com
Printed in the USA
FSOW01n0652190416
19410FS